Dear Reader, September 2019

I hope you enjoy every word of every story. 12/19

Sid Kelly.

GOOD OLD
UNCLE SAM
AND OTHER
SHORT STORIES

by

SID KELLY

Order this book online at www.trafford.com
or email orders@trafford.com

Most Trafford titles are also available at major online book retailers.

Print information available on the last page.

ISBN: 978-1-4907-9553-9(sc)
ISBN: 978-1-4907-9552-2 (hc)
ISBN: 978-1-4907-9554-6 (e)

Library of Congress Control Number: 2019907220

Trafford rev. 06/11/2019

www.trafford.com

North America & international
toll-free: 1 888 232 4444 (USA & Canada)
fax: 812 355 4082

CONTENTS

GOOD OLD UNCLE SAM

THE YEAR WAS 2015. The place was a small village thirty miles outside of Lyon, France. The family of Mr. Joe Walker had gotten together the day after Joe's funeral. The Walker family was gathered in what used to be Joe's home. Joe's wife, Brigitte, had died three years before, but their two daughters and son, along with all seven grandchildren, were there. The four youngest grandchildren were sitting apart from everyone else and talking about their grandpa Joe. The subject came up of the stories he used to tell. After the four had talked for a while, Claude, the eldest of the four, took over.

"My favorite story was the one where Grandpa killed twenty-two Germans, including nine Gestapo officers at the end of Second World War."

His mother, on hearing this, said, "He killed nine Gestapo officers? Aren't you making that one up?"

"No, Mum, honest. Grandpa told me this about two months ago."

"What exactly did he tell you?" his mother asked.

"He said the year was 1945, and the Germans knew they were going to lose the war. D-Day had happened three weeks before, and the Germans were on the retreat. Because Grandpa was working with the French underground, he knew exactly where most of the Gestapo officers lived. But until then their houses had been so well guarded, it was too dangerous to try anything. But now panic had set in. The Germans were in a hurry to get out of France and back to Germany. The French Resistance thought the time was ripe for some bold action. So dressed as a Gestapo officer, Grandpa drove in a stolen Gestapo officer's car to each of the nine houses. At each house he knocked on the front door and, using his impeccable German, asked for the officer, saying he had an urgent message for him. After being let into the house, he shot the officer and any other Germans that were there. In some houses, there were French maids and butlers. He didn't shoot them because he knew that with the war coming to an end, they wouldn't talk. He did this in all nine houses, killing a total of twenty-two people. That's what he told me, Mum."

"I know it's an appealing story," said his mother. "But because he spoke impeccable German and was wearing a German uniform and drove an officer's car, do you think for one moment they would allow a black man to walk into the house?"

"Gee, Mum, that never crossed my mind." Now Claude's feelings were hurt. Did Grandpa go to his grave after having lied to me? Claude wondered. As it turned out, Grandpa's story was based on a true story, but at a different time and place. What had happened in the true story was distasteful, to say the least. So Grandpa told Claude the story the way he did so he would appear a hero, not a villain. To know about the events that were the cause of the original story, and the true story itself, one has to go back to Grandpa's early life.

Joe Walker's original named was Terry Packham. He was born in the state of Mississippi, USA, in 1922. He was born in a small farmhouse, which boasted ten acres of arable land with a few trees on its periphery. His father was a sharecropper, and his mother taught at an all-black school. *Brown vs. Board of Education* (1954) was still thirty-three years away. Terry grew up in a very happy and unique environment; it was loving and educationally oriented. Because his mother spoke French and Spanish, Terry became proficient in both these languages by the time he was ten. The education he received from his father was completely different. But to a boy growing up in a rural area, what his father taught him was far more fun than learning languages. His father taught him how to shoot and hunt. By the time Terry was twelve, he was a better shot than his father with both pistol and rifle. With his scope rifle, he could drop a deer at half a mile. His parents were very proud of their precocious only child.

Socially he got on well with his peers in their black neighborhood. The only time he felt any discomfort in his life was when he went into town and had to deal with the white folks, which fortunately wasn't very often. His parents had told him over and over again, Keep out of trouble. Just keep to yourself and mind your own business. Don't ever look a white person in the eye and whatever you do, don't ever stare at a white woman. Some white folks were okay, but others would make trouble for the slightest reason. The town was small, with a population of about 300, with a third of the population being black. As in other urban Southern towns, black and white populations lived in distinctly segregated areas. His father was a master at dealing with white folks. He was always polite and cheerful and never looked them directly in the face. When he went into town, he would sell his fresh produce at prices lower than anyone else's. Because everyone was happy with Mr. Packham, Terry was never bothered when he went into town, not like some of the other boys were. Their 10-acre farm was bought by Joe's grandfather in 1867 during the reconstruction period after the Civil War. So the Packham family had been selling their farmed produce to nearby and surrounding towns for nearly seventy years, and it seemed as if Terry was next in line to carry on this family tradition.

But one day something happened that changed everything for the Packham family and for nearly everyone else in the world. On December 7, 1941, Japan attacked Pearl Harbor. America declared war on Japan, and soon after Germany declared war on America. Immediately America needed volunteers for its armed services. Signs were everywhere saying, "Your Country Needs You!" Terry was taken in. He wanted to serve his country. He couldn't wait to get down to the local recruiting station and sign up. His parents were appalled at the thought of their only son going into the army. The American armed forces are segregated, they told him. All the officers are white, just as it was in WWI and the Civil War. Whatever his parents said was of no avail. He'd made his mind up. He wanted to serve. So he enlisted. From the very first moment Terry loved army life.

Terry was posted to Fort Bragg, North Carolina, to do his basic training. Fort Bragg is the largest military installation in the world. It is located in four counties, covering 251 square miles. It is also the home of the famous Eighty-second Airborne Division. Terry had heard all sorts of stories about how difficult and grueling basic training was and that cruel, sadistic, white sergeants would forever be shouting out stupid orders. None of it fazed Terry. In fact, Terry was sorry when the basic training was over. He was top of his class in everything: shooting, running, climbing, crawling, self-defense, and written tests; and when it came to languages, no one else came close to speaking three languages. No one was as smart and as able as Terry. Perhaps that's why he loved it. Then one day, when everyone was sitting around talking and trying to guess where and when they were going to be shipped out, in walked the command sergeant major. Now the command sergeant major is the second-highest rank in the whole American army after the sergeant major of the army. Everyone jumped to attention at the double. The privates had only ever seen him once before, and that was from a distance. The highest rank they'd ever dealt with before was their sergeant, who was six ranks below the man now standing front of them.

"I want everyone out," said the command sergeant major, "except Private Packham." "Yes, sir," they all shouted. The place was empty in seconds.

I wonder what this is all about, Terry thought.

"I take it you're Private Terry Packham?"

"Yes, sir," Terry quickly and respectfully replied.

"You're to take all your personal belongings and come with me. Leave your army uniform here. You won't need it. Take everything, because you won't be coming back."

"Yes, sir." Terry quickly packed his few belongings and left without being able say goodbye to his newly made friends. The other privates must have been wondering what the hell was going on as they saw Terry walking behind the command sergeant major toward the VIP building. Terry was led up to the top floor to the office of the sergeant major of the army. Joe couldn't believe it. He was going into the office of the top man in the American army. The command sergeant major opened the door and announced that Private Packham was here.

"Thank you," a loud voice answered. "Let him in and close the door to leave us in private."

"Yes, sir," said the command sergeant major, who was also wondering what the hell was going on.

"Come in and sit down, Private Packham. Make yourself comfortable."

"Yes, sir," said Terry.

"I have an address here that you have to report to in three days' time. It's in Washington, DC, and you must be there promptly for a meeting at 9:00 am."

"Yes, sir."

"Don't ask me what this is about because I haven't a clue. All I know is it's right from the top—the president himself."

"Wow!" exclaimed Terry.

"Here's more than enough money for you to fly to Washington, stay in a hotel for a few nights, and have a few relaxing days before you report in. Those were my orders to give to you. And good luck to whatever it is you're going to do."

"Thank you, sir."

"And one last thing."

"Yes, sir."

"Not a word to anyone—that includes your family and anyone else who is breathing on this planet. Got it?"

"Yes, sir."

From the gist of what the sergeant major of the army had told him, Terry believed he was going to have a personal interview. But when he arrived at the address given to him, he was surprised to find there were thirty or so people already there. By the time it was 9:00 a.m., the room was full with about a hundred people: most were white, three were black, and one was Hispanic.

At about one minute past nine, a casually dressed man walked in and closed the door behind him. He made his way to the lectern and asked everyone to take a seat. He began by telling everyone that he worked for an intelligence agency that Terry and probably most of the others had never heard of before. Then he said, "Because you have highly proven yourself during your basic training, you have been selected as candidates for a special secret mission. But before I go any further, if there's anyone here who wants to decline this opportunity, please say so now?" Obviously no one did. He then explained, "To fight the Nazis, the British have set up a special unit separate from their regular armed forces. Uncle Sam is going to help them out in doing this. By this time next week, you'll all be in England with an umbrella over your head while learning about the many ways you can kill a Nazi." This got a laugh, but at the same time everyone got the point.

As they were told, a week later Terry was in England training. The one hundred men were divided up into four groups and sent to different locations. The first thing that happened was everybody was given a new identity and issued a new passport. They could give themselves a new name or one would be allocated to them. Terry always liked walking, so he gave himself the surname Walker. For his first name, he chose Joe after his lifelong hero, Joe Lewis, the present black heavyweight boxing champion of the world. So during the war, he was known as Joe Walker, who would operate in a unit that hardly anyone knew about. Because it was so hush-hush, only the president and some of his closest aides knew of its existence. A bit like Vice President Truman not knowing about the Manhattan Project that developed the atomic bomb. All records of Joe's basic training were erased, so Terry Packham no longer officially existed. Joe Walker, the partisan, secretly existed throughout the duration of the war and, as events would dictate, Joe Walker would be his name for the majority of his remaining life.

Again, Joe loved every minute of the training. The training in England was nowhere as physical as his US Army basic training, but he found it far more interesting. He learned all sorts of things that were to be both useful and lifesaving. He learned how to break into and start vehicles, use Morse code, set explosives, make and detect booby traps, pick locks, operate a radio, derail and blow up trains or vehicles, became familiar with many types of firearms, parachuting into fields and wooded areas, become skilled at driving motorbikes and cars, learned the art of disguise, became competent at remembering information (names and addresses), and had classes in speaking and writing German, which he practiced and perfected throughout the war.

The training was very thorough and lasted six months. The big day finally came, and he was called into the office for a debriefing.

Joe and three others were to be dropped behind enemy lines in France. They were to work with the French underground and give them all the support they could. This was no surprise to Joe because of his fluency in French. When Joe got into the routine of French partisan life, he couldn't believe how accepted he was. He was a black man whom the French partisans accepted without the slightest prejudice. The girls not only eagerly took up conversations with him, they wanted to go to bed with him. Now these girls were no sluts or whores or anything like that. These were well-educated, hardworking, good French citizens. Often, after he had made love to a white French woman, he thought, *If this was Mississippi, I would be lynched.* Compared to the hick town he had come from, Joe felt he was now living in an advanced open-minded society.

So started three and a half years of partisan killing and sabotaging against a formidable enemy. Most of the time, Joe, and whoever he was working with, had the advantage. Whether it was an assassination or a sabotage, they would first survey the surrounding area and, if satisfied, it would be they who chose when to strike. Most of the time, things went well for them. They would be in and out before there was any chance of pursuit. Joe was always in the thick of it. He frequently derailed trains that were carrying Gestapo officers and would follow up by shooting them at close blank range or at a distance with his scope rifle. Sometimes, when a very high-ranking German official was being transported by train, the Gestapo would run another train in front of the one the high official was on. This would make it difficult to use the derail method of assassination. Also such high officials were very difficult to assassinate when traveling by car because they were escorted and surrounded by many cars. But the weak link in the transportation of high-ranking Gestapo officers was when he walked from the car to the train between two lines of guards. Even when the guards were shoulder to shoulder, there was that moment when the high-ranking official's head passed between the heads of two of the guards. This fraction of a second was enough for Joe. He would pick him off just as he picked off squirrels as a kid with his scoped rifle. The Gestapo were flummoxed. They just didn't know what to do except round up more people and execute them. Even Hitler inquired why so many of his top men in that area of Paris were being assassinated. Another specialty of Joe's was he would imitate being a laborer. He would dress shabbily, make himself dirty, and walk through towns and villages carrying sacks of vegetables. He would stop in bars and have a beer with the locals. All the time he would be scanning the area, noting car checkpoints, the activities and numbers of soldiers, who it was that seemed overfriendly with the Germans, and anything which could be used for later operations. And just as he'd acquired the knack as a kid with the white folks back at home, he could be obsequious with Germans to just the right degree. It was a balance between making the Germans feel respected and not being thought of as fools.

Although the war saw savage fighting in many parts of the world, such as the Russian front and Japanese jungle warfare, France never saw such fighting because it was occupied. And because of the occupation, some Frenchmen and women ingratiated themselves to the Germans, which increased the possibility of the underground being infiltrated. Because of infiltration or a captured partisan talking under torture, underground safe houses were occasionally raided by the Gestapo. If the partisans knew someone had been captured, they would cancel all plans and vacate the area. Because of the possible danger of being taken prisoner, the partisans carried cyanide tablets to commit suicide. A trick that Joe had up his sleeve was he never stayed in safe houses because he always slept outside. He'd learned how to do this in the early years of his life when he went hunting with his father. This saved his life four times during surprise raids. Two of the raids had only two cars and six men. These were easily dealt with, and no partisan lives were lost. The other two raids had such a large number of German soldiers that Joe melted into the night and many lives were lost. This brought about the sad fact that anyone anytime could get killed. It was the nature of the business. So as much as you relied on and got to like someone, it was understood that that someone could be removed from your life within a second. This bothered Joe somewhat, because he'd become very friendly with a female French partisan named Brigitte. But so far so good. Both were safe. The war ground on, and on June 6, 1944,

D-Day arrived. From then on, the Germans were packing bags and in retreat. This became a very busy time for Joe, as there were lots of old scores to settle.

With the Germans retreating, and knowing that American and British soldiers would soon be in Paris, the French population became bolder. They gave the partisans more information than they'd ever had before, such as names of who had helped the Germans and where Germans would gather together to socialize. How many Germans and spies Joe killed is unknown. He didn't even know himself. There were untold numbers of train derailments, factories, and army barracks blown up, and restaurants and bars where Germans and their wives used to socialize were blown up, sniping assassinations and many other operations. Many men and some women were decorated for bravery in the war. Such brave acts could be for carrying a wounded comrade to safety or overrunning a German machine gun nest. But then there were people like Joe. He spent three and a half years killing hundreds of Germans and saving so many lives and he received no recognition because what he did was top secret. The only people who knew were the people he'd worked with. They would all say he was a legend in his own time. There was no one else who came close to Joe Walker. He was in a league of his own.

Before flying back to England for debriefing and demobilization, Joe had a long talk with Brigitte. They agreed they'd had wonderful times together during the war. But the reality of Brigitte living in the boondocks of Mississippi or Joe living in France with his ailing mother still living in the US was just not practical. They bid a sad farewell and promised to keep in touch. Joe flew to England and was debriefed and demobilized. His old passport was returned to him. He was given a new army uniform and flew back to the USA on September 1945 as Private Terry Packham. It wasn't until 1948 that President Truman signed the law that desegregated the US Armed Forces.

Terry flew into Jackson Airport, Mississippi. From there he took a three-hour train ride to his out-in-the-middle-of-nowhere town, Walnut Buff. From there he planned to get a cab to his farm and meet up with his mum, whom he'd not seen for nearly four years. But before doing that, he went into the local store and bought some flowers and milk chocolates for her. His mum loved milk chocolates. As he came out of the store, he was accosted by three white teenagers who blocked his path. "What have we got here," one of them arrogantly said. "I think we got us here an uppity nigger all neatly dressed in his army uniform. What do you say to that, nigger?"

"Oh, I think you've made a mistake, young man. My name is not Nigger; it's Terry." And with a big smile on his face, Terry extended his right hand and said, "What's your name, boy? I'd like to be your friend."

They'd never before experienced such a well-spoken, cool, calm, and collected nigger. They were taken completely by surprise. They didn't know what to do. They couldn't shake hands with a nigger, but they couldn't back off. So they did what they always did with local niggers who didn't know their place. They were going to beat the living daylights out of him. The two front boys then rushed at Terry. The one that had done all the talking was slightly in front of the other. There was a *wham* from nowhere, and the first boy was down and out. The second boy, who saw what had happened, was already in motion and couldn't stop going forward. *Wham*, he too was down and out. The third boy backed off and couldn't believe his eyes. He was the younger of the three, and up until this moment, he'd thought his two friends were invincible. But there they were, stone-cold out on the ground. They were not even moving or twitching. It was like Joe Lewis hitting someone who'd never boxed before.

Terry went to the cab station. Two white drivers wouldn't take him, but the third cab with a black driver did. "You're the late Mr. Packham's son," said the driver.

"Yes," said Terry.

"I'm sorry to hear about your dad passing. He was a good man."

"Thank you," Terry said.

"I know the address. We'll be there before you know it," said the driver.

"How are things around here?" Terry asked.

"Nothing's changed. A few of the whites that signed up were killed in the war. And seeing you coming back all healthy and intact may be a reason for some of them to cause trouble, if you know what I mean? Just be careful," advised the driver.

"Thanks for the advice," said Terry. They rounded the corner and saw his wonderful mother waiting for him. Not wanting to upset his mother on their first day together, Terry never mentioned what had happened in town. The next day, he told his mother he thought they should do their weekly shopping in Fairfax County an hour's ride away. He thought it would be safer. "Also, while we're over there, we can drop in and see your sister."

"Okay, Terry," his mum said. "You know best." And that's what they did for about five or six weeks. Then Terry's mum took a turn for the worst and was laid up in bed. They needed groceries and a few other things, so Terry decided to risk it and nip into town. He didn't want to leave his mother alone for too long, so it would be quicker for him to ride into town than going to Fairfax County. When he got to town, everything appeared nice and peaceful. He quickly did his shopping, and as he came out of the local store, he was not met by three teenagers as before, but by a crowd of at least twenty people. Terry saw the original three in the crowd. The crowd, mostly teenagers, was egging on a teenager who was blocking his path. He was huge, white, 6 feet 6 inches tall, and must have weighed 300 pounds.

Now Terry wasn't the least bit fazed with any of this. In fact, he thought, *I'm going to have a bit of fun before I get around to sorting this out.* The hulk then spoke. "So you're the uppity nigger I've heard so much about." The hulk was expecting some sort of answer that he could twist around to start a fight. But what he heard instead was, "I know you're here to beat the shit out of me, but can I know your name before you do it?"

"I'm Bill," said the hunk.

"Okay, Bill, why do you want to do this?"

"Because, nigger, you beat two of my best friends up."

"No. I never beat them up. I just punched them once, and it was all over. Now honestly, Bill, is that beating someone up?"

Bill couldn't play these word games. He just wanted to set an example with this nigger and be a hero in front of his friends. But before he could say or do anything, Terry said to him, "Before you do whatever it is you are going to do to me, Bill, may I ask you a question?"

"Sure," said Bill. "Fire away because when I've finished with you, you're not going to be talking very much for a while."

"Well thanks, Bill, I'll remember that. Have you ever heard of James Jeffries?"

"No. Should I? Does he live around here?"

"No, no, Bill. You're not up with your American boxing history, are you? About fifty-plus years ago, James Jeffries used to be the heavyweight boxing champion of the world."

"So what?" exclaimed Bill.

"Well, he was persuaded to come out of retirement to fight the heavyweight champion of that time. The champion's name was Jack Johnson, and he was the first black man to hold the title. And have you any idea what the newspapers all over the world referred to him as?"

"I haven't a clue, and I couldn't care less," retorted Bill.

Unperturbed, Terry continued. "They called him the Great White Hope. And you, Bill, remind me of the Great White Hope."

"Oh yer, why's that?"

"Well, for this crowd, you're their Great White Hope. They're hoping you can kick my ass, just as they hoped James Jeffries would kick Jack Johnson's ass. But I'm sorry to tell you, Bill, Jack Johnson kicked James Jeffries' ass. He kicked his ass so bad that they turned the cameras off. So I'm wondering, because you're the Great White Hope of today, what you're going to do to this smart-assed nigger standing in front of you?"

By now Terry and Bill had verbally sparred for about three minutes, and the crowd was getting restless and impatient. Bill sensed this and said to Terry, "I tell you what I'm going to do. I'm going to knock so many teeth down your throat you'll need dentures."

But before Bill had chance to move, Terry quickly stepped forward so their fronts were nearly touching. He then looked up into Bill's face and, with the biggest smile he could throw, said, "Go ahead, Mr. Great White Hope, I'm waiting."

But because Terry had stepped in so close, there was no space for Bill to swing a punch. So Bill began to step back on his right foot to make some space so he could throw a punch. But the instant he began to step back, he felt a powerful force hit him in the testicles. When Terry's knee sharply and accurately struck the intended target, all Bill's desire to fight left him. The excruciating pain he felt buckled him up. As Bill buckled, his head came down and Terry pole-axed him with a well-placed punch on the jaw. Bill was down and lights were out.

The crowd, which was previously jeering, suddenly went silent with disbelief. They really thought this giant teenager was going to put this nigger in his place. Now they realized this was not going to happen. So with strength in numbers, the crowd surged forward to take care of this uppity nigger. There were a few policemen and blacks watching, but they never got involved. Then with the supposedly speed of Wyatt Earp, Terry suddenly had a Colt 45 in his right hand. The crowd drew back. "The nigger's got a gun."

"No, you're wrong," shouted Terry. "The nigger's got two guns," and he pulled out another gun with his left hand. "And I'm ambidextrous," he added.

"What's that mean?" someone shouted.

"It means I'm able to use both hands equally well, and I never miss at close quarters. So let's all keep calm and no harm will come to any of you." The crowd melted away as he walked to his car. But just as he reached his car, someone shouted, "We know where you live, nigger." Then more voices joined in and repeated, "Yer, we know where you live, nigger."

Although Terry's mother was unwell, as soon as he got home Terry told her, "Pack your things, Mum, you're going to stay with your sister for a while. I'll explain why in the car." Terry dropped his mother off and went straight back home. He packed some clothing and enough food and drink for a couple of days. He drove to a wooded area on the edge of his property and hid his car. He then walked about half a mile to another wooded area on his property and climbed nearly to the top of a tree. At the top of the tree was a treehouse that he and his father had built when he was a kid. It needed some repair, but it was good enough to sleep in and far enough away from the house. With his mother out of the way, he now needed a few quiet days to think things out.

On his second day in the tree, he saw three cars pull up in front of the house. Through his binoculars, he saw six men encircle and enter the house. After a while they came out and stood by their cars talking. He recognized most of them. They were about his age. This meant to Terry that the teenagers had sought help. Because of his mother, he was unsure what to do. Without her, he would have caught the next plane out of the country. Still hoping it would all blow over, he slept at night in the treehouse. During the day, he carefully made his way to the house and got more things. Upon leaving, he splashed a mixture of chemicals all around the house and behind him on the way back to the treehouse. The next day, the same three cars came back with the same six men. But this time the men had dogs with them. They took the dogs all around the house to see if they could pick up a scent. But they couldn't because of the chemicals Terry had put down.

The cars drove away, but one returned and parked about half a mile away from the house. Using the scopes on his high-powered rifle, he could see the car. It remained most of the day before it left. This told Terry that this wasn't going to blow over so quickly. What was he to do? It was a waste of time going to the police. That was a joke. Twelve white male jurors was standard practice in black trials in Mississippi. But he hadn't committed any crime. He had licenses for his guns, and all the fighting he was involved in was done in self-defense. But he knew none of this mattered. So he decided to stay in the treehouse and think how he and his mother could safely move out of the state of Mississippi. But an event took place that quickly cancelled out any plans of moving.

Two days later at least six cars came to the house with a dozen or so men. They all seemed jubilant and many of them had rifles. He recognized some of the men. He had known them since he was a kid. Their looks had changed with the passing of time, but he still knew who they were. Then about half an hour later, three more cars came with about ten more men with more guns. Again he recognized some of them. *What were they up to?*, Terry wondered. Some of the men had gone into the house. Others were just standing around outside chatting and drinking beer. No one was scanning the area with binoculars as they had done on previous visits. Nor were there any dogs this time. They just all seemed to be waiting around for something. It wasn't long before Terry found out what it was. All of a sudden those inside the house came running out in great excitement as another car pulled up in front of the house. A loud cheer went up from everyone when they saw the car. Terry, who was looking through the scope of his high-powered rifle, couldn't quite make out what was going on because there were so many people crowding around the car.

But finally, when he saw the reason for their excitement, he nearly dropped his rifle. To say Terry was horrified by what he saw limits the ability of adjectives to describe emotions. They had his mother gagged and bound. Terry hadn't a clue how they'd located her, and he would probably never find out. He couldn't hear what they were saying from a distance of 500 yards, but he could see they were taunting her. What they were saying, Terry could only guess. But the big question for him was, What did they intend to do to his mother? And what could he do about the situation? After about five minutes, the excitement had subsided. All Terry could see was crowded circles of men focusing on the center of the circles they had formed. He couldn't see his mother, but he knew she was their focal point. Her body suddenly appeared in sight in the center of the circle. Someone had lifted her up above the heads of the circles of men. And there she stayed because she was standing on something. Suddenly, he saw and realized what was about to happen.

A noose was encircled around her neck. They're going to lynch my mother, Terry wailed out. Those fucking son of bitches. This is the sort of thing the Nazis did, but then there was a war going on. Then he realized it was 1946, and there was still a war going in the USA. It was a war between bigoted whites and those trying to improve the human rights of blacks. These bigoted whites were especially now shitting their pants because emancipated blacks were now demanding the same civil rights and voting rights as whites.

Terry had been in this situation before, but with a difference. This situation included his mother. He'd often witnessed partisan friends being captured by the Nazis. He knew the routine: torture then execution. Today, he knew he could go in with guns blazing. He would have killed a few, but then he would have been killed. During the war there had been endless hours of discussion on this subject. The verdict was always reluctantly the same. The captured are going to die. But those that can remain alive can seek revenge for those that died. But it was his mother they were stringing up. He didn't want to look, but he had to. They had kicked away the chair and her body was now quivering. The crowd was shouting out taunts and those closest to her were swinging her body backward and forward. Terry turned away. He couldn't do anything to solve the problem. If he'd gone down there shooting, he would have been shot and killed, and his mother would still have been lynched. Or if he had gone down and given himself up, they would have lynched him anyway and who knows what before that. And they would still have probably lynched his mother. So Terry sat there in the treehouse and cried and cried for hours on what was the worst day of his life.

Finally, Terry heard the cars leave. His mother's body was hanging motionless at the end of a rope tied to the oak tree in front of the house. As upset as he was, his training and experiences told him not to go down to the crime scene. They were going to be watching the house. They knew that most people would be emotionally drawn to cutting a lynched mother down to bury her. But Terry was not on the list of most people.

Now that his mother was dead, Terry Packard reverted back to his war name Joe Walker. Joe stayed in the treehouse for a few days and came up with a plan. Now for a plan to work when the odds are heavily against you, the plan must be bold and daring. But most of all it has to be ingenious. It had be a such plan that no one in their right mind would ever think of carrying it out. During the war, making such plans was Joe's specialty. The plan was simple and daring and had to do with the now-defunct Ku Klux Klan (KKK). The clan was a white supremacist group, and there were still a few nutcases around who believed in the superiority of the Anglo-Saxon race. These individuals were not usually found in cosmopolitan cities. They were found mostly in the rural areas of Southern states such as where Joe had been born and raised. In fact, his mother's sister, Aunt Ruth, told him every now and again men drove around Joe's town dressed in KKK uniforms. Paradoxically, this would help Joe's plan. The first thing Joe needed was some white sheets to make a KKK outfit.

Taking no chances, Joe drove two hours to a shopping mall that was in the opposite direction from his town. There he purchased some white bedsheets, some sticks of dynamite, and groceries for a week. He also stole a three-year-old Chevy, which was fully tanked, from the shopping mall carpark. When he got back to the treehouse, he set to work in making the KKK outfit. After a few days, he was all set to put his plan into action. Having grown up in such a small town, everyone knew where everyone else lived. So Joe knew exactly which houses to go to. His daring plan was simple. He would knock on the door of the selected house dressed in his KKK outfit and ask if he could come in. He would wear white gloves so no one would see his black hands. He chose Saturday morning for his plan because on this day most of the women went shopping in the surrounding towns. The streets in the white residential area were usually very quiet, which was what Joe was banking on. He parked the stolen car just outside the residential area. He then proceeded by foot and knocked on the door of the first house. A man opened the door and Joe recognized him. He was there at his mother's lynching. Using his perfected white man's accent, he asked if he could come in as he had a message from the Klan. "Sure, come on in," the man said. It was important that Joe got inside the house because he couldn't kill him outside without attracting attention. Then he had to find out if anyone else was in the house. So he said, "Sorry to bother you, is there anyone else home?"

"No," the man replied. After Joe had removed the hood and revealed his smiling black face, his gun quickly appeared from nowhere. Then a well-placed shot left a clean hole in the man's forehead. During the era of lynching, if a lynching had anything to do with a white woman, a black man would have his penis cut off and stuffed into his mouth. Because this was a lynching and it had to do with a woman, a special, kind, and loving woman—his mother—Joe cut off the man's penis and stuffed it into the dead man's mouth. Joe thought, *Whether I end up dead or alive, this town isn't going to forget my mother's lynching.*

Joe went from house to house. At some houses, nobody was home. Some had a man or men he didn't recognize. There he told them about the Monday night Klan meeting at 8:00 am. When asked what the meeting was about, he just smiled and said, "Sorry, I really don't know." At a couple of houses, a person's mother or/and a sister were at home with a man he recognized from the lynching. In such cases, the women became collateral damage. At one house a man was so nervous that he wailed and urinated in fear. Seizing the opportunity, he told the man he would spare his life if he could tell him how they found his mother. He blurted out, "It was Mary. She lives three houses down the street. She saw your mother shopping with another woman. Mary followed them and found out where she was staying." Joe killed the wailing man anyway. The Golden Rule: no witnesses. At the third house down the street, Mary was there with a man who was at the lynching. Joe told them why he was there and it was now their turn. He delivered two more well-placed bullets. All in all, Joe executed nine men he'd recognized at the lynching, along with four other men and six women. He now had one more score to settle. Making his way to the center of town, and still dressed in his KKK outfit, he let himself in through the side door of the KKK building. It was an old building and now rarely frequented by the general public. But some of the old-timers used to hang out there bullshitting about the old days. He found four of them. They were quite happy to see someone enter the building wearing a Klan outfit. But when Joe removed the hood, exposing his black face with a big smile of white shiny teeth and brandishing a Colt 45 in his right hand, they knew their days were over. After adding four more to his list, he put the hood back on and strategically placed sticks of dynamite throughout the building. He then quickly left the building using the same side door. He got back to his car just as the KKK building exploded.

Up until now, everything had gone according to plan. But when Joe got into the car and removed the hood, a couple of men saw him. They sounded the alarm, jumped into their car, and gave chase. Fortunately for Joe, nobody heard or took any notice of them. In two minutes, both cars were out of town and on country roads. Joe now used one of his favorite tricks. He drove at medium speed to let the chasing car catch up with him but not pass him. This made the chasing driver frustrated, so he ended up tailgating Joe's car. This is exactly what Joe wanted. With the driver's side window open, Joe lit one of his sticks of dynamite. Because timing was critical, Joe waited a few seconds before he threw the stick of dynamite back toward the chasing car. As soon as he threw the stick of dynamite, he put his foot down hard on the gas. The stick landed on the chasing car's bonnet and exploded just as it bounced on to the windshield. The two passengers were blown to smithereens and what was left of the car overturned and came to rest on the side of the road. At the moment of explosion, Joe's car was far enough away not to be affected by the blast. Joe had revenged his mother and now had one more thing to do before leaving the country. He had to bury his mother. He decided to do it right now while the town was in disarray. He quickly made his way home and cut his mother down. He then dug a grave next to his father's grave and buried his mother. He said a few prayers and then he was off. There was no time to hang around.

During the war Joe had taken the precaution of having extra passports made. He intuitively felt that one day they would be useful. And this was the day. He had British, French, and Spanish passports in his war name of Joe Walker. His plan was to drive north from Mississippi up to the Canadian border. From there he would drive to Quebec and catch a plane to Sweden. From Sweden, he would rent a car and drive to the outskirts of Paris and meet up with Brigitte. This roundabout route was taken in case they were alerts for him at any of the main US airports and the Paris airport. But before he could do this, there was one snag he had to take care of. During the war he had grown a beard and a mustache. And this was how the pictures in the passports looked, with him having a beard and a mustache. So in the meanwhile, he disguised himself with a false beard and mustache while he was growing new ones, which he guessed would take two to three weeks.

Meanwhile, the authorities in town were not sitting idly around. Because the sheriff, nor anyone else, could locate Terry, he call the armed services in Washington. He had a friend, Greg, who worked in the army records department who might be able to give him a clue to where Terry had absconded to. A couple of days later, Greg called back to check up on the information he'd been given about Terry. The information was correct, but there were no records. "There must be some mistake," said the sheriff. "There's a man in town who worked in the enlisting office during the war, and he remembers Terry Packham enlisting."

"Okay," Greg said, "I'll take another look." A few days later, he got back to the sheriff. "No luck," he said. "Not a trace. But there is one thing. If this Terry Packham was in top priority secret service, his records would be classified and closed to the public for thirty years."

The sheriff was persistent. "This guy has killed a lot of people? Doesn't that mean anything?"

"I'm not sure, but I don't think so. Why did he kill a lot of people?" Greg asked.

For a moment, the sheriff was silent. Then he said, "His mother was lynched a few days ago."

"Wow," said Greg. "This is 1946. I thought you guys in the South had stopped doing things like that."

"Well, we have," said the sheriff, "but he really pissed off a lot of people."

"Do you have any proof for what he did? Have you any witnesses or evidence?"

"Well, no. But it must have been him. Only someone with special training could have killed so many people."

"So he killed some people. How many people did he kill?" Greg asked.

"Twenty-one," said the sheriff.

"Wow!" said Greg. "But even with twenty-one bodies, if you don't have any evidence, you can't charge him," Greg said. "If I were you, I would forget the whole thing. Your town took on more than it could handle. It seems to me that this Terry Packham is a very special person. Although you and I go back a long way, please don't bother me again on this." Greg then put the phone down without waiting for any further comments from the sheriff.

> *Isn't it strange,* Joe thought, *in wartime, the more people you kill in state-sponsored murders, the greater the hero you become. In peacetime, if you murder just one person, even if that person is known to be a threat to society, you set in motion a huge train of events, all paid for by the American taxpayer. Police from all forty-eight states know every detail about you. Then when you're apprehended, the bureaucracy set in motion would require many tall trees of paperwork to keep the judicial system oiled, including the prosecuting and defense attorneys and their staff, judges, and all the people staffing the courts. Then if you're convicted, you're off to prison to be executed or serve life. If executed, there's a team of people who specialize in putting the guilty party*

> *to death. When they're doing their state duty, they're filmed and watched by an audience of attorneys, reporters, and relatives. If given life, the guilty person has to deal with prison guards, prison food, prison rules, prison gangs, and sometimes solitary confinement. All of this because he took one life. In wartime, one more dead body wouldn't cause an eye blink. Yes, it's really strange,* Joe thought.

So Joe drove north to upstate New York and lay low for a few weeks in Port Jarvis. It was an old town that had once been a canal and railroad transportation center. It was a quiet town. A perfect place to lay low and let some hair grow. While there he disposed the guns and dynamite. For security reasons, he didn't sell them. He dumped them into a lake. It took three weeks before he again looked like the photos in the passports. The journey was flawless. He passed through all the checkpoints without raising any suspicion. In Quebec, he spoke to the official at the passport check-in for several minutes. They even cracked jokes in French with each other. Such was Joe's gift for languages.

After meeting up with Brigitte, they decided it would be safer to move away from the Paris area. So using connections of a very trusted friend from the French underground, they selected the suburbs of Lyon, France's second-largest city. There they married and settled down. Like his mother before him, Joe ended up being a teacher teaching French and English. Brigitte was a busy mother raising three children, two girls and a boy. Although family life was hectic, they always made a point of vacationing every year in a foreign country. During their lifetime, they traveled to most of Europe, the Middle East, the Far East, Africa, India, Australia, and New Zealand. Brigitte, perhaps influenced by Joe, never wanted to go to the Americas. And they never did.

From their three children came the joys of seven grandchildren. It was a two-way loving street. Everyone loved everyone else. The big event of most weeks was when they met at their grandparents' house. As the years passed by, the cycle of life visited the Walker family, as it does everyone. Brigitte was diagnosed with pancreatic cancer and passed away six months later. Three years later, Joe was ailing from nothing in particular except old age. He'd slowed down and didn't have much energy. His sight and hearing were in decline, and he now hardly ever left the house. His mind was still sharp and active. He spent most of his time listening to the news and reminiscing about his past. The year was 2015 and a lot had happened since Joe had left the army in 1945.

One day Joe was feeling unwell and laid down to rest. While resting he began to reminisce. His thoughts followed no chronological order and jumped from subject to subject. Such were his thoughts: I'm so glad I came back to France. I've had a wonderful life with Brigitte. France, or anywhere else, isn't perfect, but it sure beats the USA as far as a black person is concerned. Because of what I did, I had to get out in 1946. But it was bad in the South in 1946. Today, there're a lot more people speaking up about racial injustices in the US and a lot more black people are now elected to high office. But racism is still in the DNA of too many Americans. Look at this guy Trump who's running for president. Any sensible person wouldn't vote for Trump if they knew about the Central Park Five and how he's treated blacks in his rental apartments. Well, American democracy has to sort him out. Look at what happened to those that were brave enough to speak up. Malcolm X, Dr. King, and Robert Kennedy—all assassinated. Then there was Rodney King. Four white policeman beat him up while twenty or more policeman just stood around watching. All on a film that went viral. What happened? The four were acquitted. No surprise to black Americans.

Most surveys on the subject say France has the best health care system in the Western world. I don't have to pay a cent for any medical expenses. I don't have any fear about going bankrupt over medical bills. Half of all bankruptcies in the US are from medical bills. As he reminisced, Joe would keep coming back to the reason why he was in France. It was Good Old Uncle Sam. Without Good Old Uncle Sam, I wouldn't have had the chance to belong to that highly classified hit squad, as Joe referred to his secret unit. Without Uncle Sam, I wouldn't have had the high standard of living that a rural black sharecropper from Mississippi could only dream about. Without Uncle Sam, I wouldn't have met Brigitte and have the loving family I have. Yes, thank you, Uncle Sam. Thank you, Good Old Uncle Sam, said Joe, as he breathed his last breath.

THAT DAMN CHARLIE

CHARLIE WHISTLED CHEERFULLY as he drove his ambulance to the last pickup of the day. He pulled up at an assisted-living complex and saw the superintendent waiting for him. "Hi, Fred, how you doing?" shouted Charlie.

"Good," Fred replied.

Charlie removed the portable stretcher from the ambulance and wheeled it through the doorway. "Which floor, Fred?"

"Floor eight, room ten. I left the door unlocked for you. His name is Mr. Blake. He's on the couch. I couldn't feel any pulse," answered Fred.

"That's okay Fred, I'll check him out." Still whistling, Charlie made his way to the elevator, up to the eighth floor and down the hallway to Room No. 10. He opened the door and was just about to wheel the stretcher in when the door opposite Room No. 10 opened. *Wow!* Charlie thought, *that's a bit of all right.* The attractive-looking woman gave Charlie a friendly smile and asked, "Are you here to take Mr. Blake away?"

Well, Charlie thought, *I'm standing here with a stretcher. She's either not too smart or wants to have a conversation with me.* But before he could say a word, the lady said, "My name is Wendy. I'm the person who told the superintendent I hadn't seen Mr. Blake for about three or four days. When the superintendent checked his room, he found Mr. Blake on the couch dead."

"Yes, that scenario seems to happen a lot," said Charlie.

"What happens now?" asked Wendy. "What will actually happen to Mr. Blake when you take him to wherever you're taking him?"

Now Charlie was a ladies' man. He was sixty years old and had never married. He had a fetching smile, dressed well, kept his hair stylish, and had the gift of the gab. He'd had several long-term relationships, numerous affairs, and was presently available. So he thought he would sidetrack his work for a while and have a short conversation with this attractive lady. "It's really very simple," Charlie confidently said. "I check him out, put him on the stretcher, put him in the ambulance, take him to the morgue, and he'll be put in a freezer where he'll be kept overnight. In the morning, they'll perform an autopsy to determine cause of death—just to make sure there was no foul play."

While this conversation was going on, Mr. Blake was lying on the couch in the living room and he could hear every word being said. Mr. Blake was supposed to be dead. But he wasn't. He couldn't move because every muscle in his body was paralyzed. But his mind was working overtime. He'd just heard this guy Charlie say he'd be taken to a morgue, and they'd perform an autopsy on him. This scared the living daylights out of him. Then he thought about that busybody pain-in-the-ass Wendy. "She's always walking around in leather kinky boots and tight-fitting jeans, which makes her rear-end look a lot larger than it already is. She's about fifty years old and always trying to look like a teenager."

At the same time Mr. Blake was having his thoughts, Charlie was thinking, *This Wendy really has a nice pair of buttocks and a very pleasant personality. I'm going to chat her up and see where it leads.* But again before he could say anything, Wendy helped him lead the conversation with a question. "Are you going to put Mr. Blake on the stretcher all by yourself? Don't you need someone to help you?"

"No. I do it all the time." With a know-it-all look on his face, Charlie said, "It's easy. Would you like to see how it's done?"

"Sure, why not?" Wendy quickly answered.

"Come on then. Follow me," said Charlie, "and close the door after you so we can have some privacy."

Charlie wheeled the stretcher over to the couch. He then showed Wendy how the stretcher's height could be adjusted so the body could easily be slid onto the stretcher. After ensuring that the stretcher's height was in the correct position, Charlie took a firm grip on Mr. Blake's left arm and leg and slid Mr. Blake from the couch on to the stretcher. "Gee, you made that look so easy," Wendy flatteringly said.

"Well, practice makes perfect," Charlie replied. "Then the last thing I do is cover him with a sheet." Which is what Charlie did. Because Charlie was so busy eyeing Wendy's firm buttocks and shapely legs and all the rest of her, he completely forgot all about the medical procedures he was supposed to perform on Mr. Blake. And instead, he turned his attention completely toward the vivacious Wendy and put his masculine charms into top gear.

As he felt his body and face being covered with the sheet, Mr. Blake began to panic. Being removed from the comfort of his couch on to the stretcher was bad enough. But after the sheet had covered his face, reality set in and he began thinking. Is this really happening to me? How am I going to get out of this? However, he realized, the first thing he mustn't do is panic. He reassured himself by thinking, I must keep calm and think of a plan. Then immediately he thought of something. It was a long shot, but it was worth trying. *When they remove the sheet from my face at the morgue, I must immediately catch their attention. I can do this if I have my eyes wide open and blinking. Then they'll know I'm alive.* Mr. Blake reasoned that of all the muscles in the body, the eyelids must be the most used. Because even when you're standing around, you're still blinking. So if they're the most used, they must be the easiest to get moving again. Whether it was true or not, he hadn't a clue. But he would give it a try. He had to because Mr. Blake couldn't think of anything else.

Charlie soon realized he didn't have to get his charms into top gear. With the way Wendy was gushing all over him, Charlie hardly needed his first gear. They were both free Saturday, so Charlie agreed to pick her up and take her out for dinner. With the business of dating taken care of, Charlie turned his attention back to Mr. Blake. Charlie put Mr. Blake in the ambulance and drove him to the hospital. At the hospital, he drove to the morgue parking area. He took the stretcher off the ambulance and wheeled Mr. Blake into the overnight freezer area. He was met by the morgue custodian.

"Hi, Sam, how are you feeling?" said Charlie.

"You know how I'm feeling, Charlie, as I always feel."

"I know," said Charlie. "You feel out of place here because you're alive and kicking and all the rest of them here are dead."

"You've got it," Sam laughed. Charlie and Sam had bantered this joke around a couple of times a week for the last four or five years. "But," said Sam, "I have to tell you Charlie, we're as busy as hell. I've never seen it so busy. What with gang violence, domestic violence, drug overdoses, opioid overdoses, hospital deaths, suicides, and don't forget our bread-and-butter, deaths by natural causes. We're literally full up with stiffs. So many stiffs that all the freezers are filled. You'll have to put yours in the operating room. He'll be the first one they cut open in the morning." After Charlie and Sam signed some paperwork, Charlie left the morgue and drove home. Once again he was whistling cheerfully. He was feeling pretty good at the moment because he was going home to watch a re-run of the *Sopranos* and tomorrow night he would see Wendy. All thoughts regarding Mr. Blake were now completely out of his mind.

Meanwhile, ever since he'd been placed on the stretcher, Mr. Blake had been trying as hard as humanly possible to open his eyes. Finally, he'd succeeded. But he was now so tired. Straining to get his eyes open had exhausted him. His plan was to rest until the sheet was removed. Then he would open his eyes and blink as much as he could. Mr. Blake had heard every word of Charlie and Sam's conversation. And the bit about him being the first one they'll cut open in the morning put a jolt of fear into him. But now the voices got fainter and he heard a door close and all was silent. *Now what?* he thought? *Am I going to lie here all night until the doctor comes? I thought someone would have checked me out by now.* Then after a while he heard some footsteps.

After Charlie had left, Sam began to think to himself. The paperwork had stated that the dead man's name was Mr. Tim Blake. *I wonder if it's the Tim Blake I went to school with? The paperwork said he was born in '45. The same year as me. Before I go home, I'm going to take a peek at this Mr. Blake. Curiosity had got the better of Sam.* He now made his way to the morgue operating room to have a look at Mr. Blake.

After hearing Sam's footsteps, Mr. Blake heard a door being unlocked. He then heard the door close, followed by footsteps heading in his direction. Although he was supposed to be dead, he could feel his heart pumping rapidly. ***Perhaps this is it***, thought Mr. Blake. ***This is my chance. I must open my eyes so whoever it is that looks*** *at me can see I'm alive. Then when he knows I'm alive, I must keep blinking.* He now had his eyes wide open. But he knew he'd only so much energy left. It was a matter of timing. Could he keep his eyes open and blinking long enough before he was looked at? All he could do was try his best. Sam made his way over to Mr. Blake and pulled back the sheet and looked at the face. It was not a face he recognized. But he was startled. He was being stared at by a couple of eyes that were huge and reminded him of an owl. Before Mr. Blake had a chance to blink, Sam quickly closed Mr. Blake's eyes and covered his face with the sheet. "That damn Charlie," Sam said, "he's supposed to take care of closing the eyes." Sam left the operating room and went home extremely irritated.

Oh no, groaned Mr. Blake to himself. *What am I going to do now?* He tried moving his hands and feet. He tried moving everything. But it was hopeless. He was exhausted from his earlier efforts. Then his mind was suddenly overcome with one consuming thought. It was dread; pure dread. *They're going to cut me open in the morning while I'm still alive. I know we all have to die, but it's how I die that concerns me.* Now he began to appreciate what people must have felt like when they were facing certain death. Death by hanging, a firing squad, the guillotine, or gassing wasn't so bad. *With these*, he thought, *death would be over before you knew it.* His mind now began to wander. He recalled his father taking him to a museum when he was a child. One of the exhibitions was a place called the Chamber of Horrors, and it was terrifying. There was an upright open coffin, which a person could be stood in. On the inside of the coffin lid were pointed rods. These were positioned so when the lid was closed, the rods would simultaneously pierce the person's head, face, chest, stomach, testicles, legs, and feet. That must have been absolutely agonizing. Then he remembered seeing a picture of a man being put to death by having his legs ripped off his body. This was done using two horses walking in opposite directions. Each horse was connected to one of the man's legs with a rope. Then when the horses were forced to walk apart, both legs were wrenched from the man's torso. *Can you imagine such horrors? Why do humans do such terrifying things to other humans?* Mr. Blake wondered to himself. Thinking of such horrors brought him back to the present moment. *What's going to happen to me?* Now he began to feel sorry for himself. He began to lament. *What have I done to deserve this? I was a good parent, an upstanding citizen, and I've never harmed anyone. Now I'm in an operating room waiting to be cut open. They want to see how I died when I'm not even dead. And I can't even scream in terror.* Once again Mr. Blake tried to be optimistic. He thought to himself, *When I'm rested up in the morning, I'll try again with the stare-and-blink routine.* That's all he could think of.

To ensure there are no mishaps in autopsy operations, all corpses are certified deceased before being placed in a freezer. This is done by a doctor who daily takes care of this procedure. When Mr. Blake was brought in late by Charlie, a mishap did occur. The freezers were all full so he was placed in the operating room ready for the morning doctors. It was they who assumed that Mr. Blake had been certified deceased. It was a long night for Mr. Blake. He didn't know what time it was, but he first heard voices then footsteps. He heard a door being unlocked and two men talking. It appeared that there was a Dr. Green and his assistant David, who the doctor addressed informally as Dave. They talked for a while then went away. *They've probably gone to prepare themselves for the day*, Mr. Blake thought.

About a quarter of an hour later, Mr. Blake heard Dr. Green say, "Okay, Dave, undress the first one. What's his name? Oh yes, Mr. Blake, and wheel him over to the slab when you're ready."

Dave came over to Mr. Blake and removed the sheet. *It seems like this man took care of himself*, Dave thought. He looks in quite good shape. Although Mr. Blake was paralyzed, he could feel Dave undressing him. Dave was taking his time because as he removed each piece of clothing, he neatly folded it and placed it on a nearby bench. Mr. Blake appreciated this slowness because he needed every second. He was desperately trying to open his eyes, but nothing was happening. Finally, all his clothes had been removed.

What would happen now? Would they wait and talk for a while before they began their business. He didn't know. But he did know that the stretcher was moving. *Come on, eyes, please open, please open*, Mr. Blake frantically said to himself. He could feel his eyes nearly open but not quite. The stretcher stopped moving and Dr. Green said, "Here, Dave, let me give you a hand." Mr. Blake's eyes were nearly open now. Just a few more seconds and they would see he was alive.

"Here we go," said the doctor, "that looks like he's in a good position for what we have to do."

Mr. Blake felt the cold steel slab against his back. His eyes just refused to open. *Oh no*, said Mr. Blake. *Now they'll never know I'm alive.*

To make matters worse, Mr. Blake now had to listen to a very frightening conversation. Dr. Green said, "Dave, I want you to perform the surgical cuts to open up the body." It was to be Dave's first time, and he was very excited. Then Dr. Green said, "Just remember, Dave, the opening has to be large enough so that I can comfortably move my hand around in order to remove body parts."

"Yes, sir, I certainly understand," said Dave. Although he had seen Dr. Green perform the procedure scores of times, and had frequently read the procedure, Dave wanted to talk himself through it just one more time before he actually started cutting. He began, "I will start with an insertion at the right shoulder followed by a cut down to the center of the chest. I will then make a mirror image cut from the left shoulder so the two cuts meet and form a V. From the point where the V meets, I will then cut a straight line down to the stomach. When finished, the cuts will look like a large Y when viewed from above the corpse's front."

Listening to Dave reciting this procedure put Mr. Blake's mental panic emotions into high alert. Simultaneously, Mr. Blake's body reacted normally from the message it received from the mind, when the mind signals that it is scared shitless.

Dave was now ready and eager to begin. He went over to Mr. Blake and stood in a comfortable position to make his first cut. Dave positioned the point of the knife on Mr. Blake's right shoulder. He paused to focus on what he was about to do when he sensed a movement. At first Dave never saw anything but just sensed something. Then he looked down and screamed out in amazement. "Holy shit!"

Dr. Green looked down and also saw the same movement. Dr. Green screamed out, "He's alive! He's alive! This has never happened before. That damn Charlie was supposed to have checked him out. He's going to dearly pay for this."

While Dave and Dr. Green were making their discoveries, Charlie and Wendy were engaged in the most popular of horizontal pleasures. Wendy was now experiencing sexual joys she had never previously experienced. As she reached the crescendo of her delights, Charlie just suddenly stopped moving. Wendy's emotions were shattered. By being suddenly denied sexual nirvana, she was both angry and confused. Angry, because her mind-blowing bliss had just hurtled from ten to zero. And confused, when Charlie's member went limp and withdrew itself from her. He then rolled over sideways onto his back and began incoherently mumbling something. Wendy quickly rolled over on to her front and screamed, "What did you say, Charlie? What did you say?"

Barely audible, Charlie said, "I'm having a heart attack." Then, with a smile on his face, and in his dying breath, he said, "What a way to go!"

About half an hour later in one of the hospital wards, Mr. Blake was comfortably in bed eating vegetable soup. He'd been injected with something that immediately brought him out of his paralyzed state. While eating his soup, he looked around the ward and was contemplating life in a completely different way. He was seeing and appreciating simple ordinary everyday things that had meant nothing to him before. There were two male patients across from his bed having a wonderful time just chatting and joking. Then in the bed next to them, a nurse was spoon feeding a patient with the vegetable soup. The look on the patient's face was screaming out thank-you. *Yes,* he reflected, *I wouldn't have given these mundane things the slightest consideration before. But this is what life's all about. Everyday ordinary things that spiritually connect human beings.*

With the thought of human beings connecting, Mr. Blake wondered how Charlie and Wendy were making out. Then Charlie's name triggered two more thoughts. *I'm here because that damn Charlie didn't do his job properly, but most important of all, I'm here because Dave saw me shitting myself.*

SMOKY AND CHUM

SMOKY AND CHUM were dogs. Smoky was a mutt and Chum was a purebred. Smoky and Chum lived about a mile from each other, but they never met, that is, except on one eventful day, which this story is about.

Describing Smoky's mixed lineage is a bit of a guess. He looked like a smaller, lighter version of a German shepherd that was cross bred with who-knows-what. The color of his coat was a shade of black, from which his owners named him Smoky. He also had a few brown streaks, noticeably on his face, legs, and tail. Chum, on the other hand, was pedigree: a Bull Terrier. His coat was white with a few black patches, and he stood about a foot high with short stocky legs. Whatever their differences, Smoky and Chum did have one thing in common. They had an affinity to a boy named Sid. Sid was about fourteen years old and used to help Bert the milkman deliver milk on weekends. And two of the streets on the milk route were streets where Smoky and Chum lived.

Sid had a close bond with Smoky but not with Chum. For several years Smoky had followed Sid around the local park and fields where Sid would hang out and play. For hours Sid would throw a stick or a ball and Smoky, like clockwork, would run and retrieve the thrown object. Then he would continually bark until Sid threw it again. During hot summer days, Sid and Smoky would sit on the grass together. Smoky would sit snugly next to Sid, and during those idyllic times Sid and Smoky needed nothing more from life. Smoky's owners were Sid's neighbors, and in those days dogs were often just let out to roam around. So for several years, Sid and Smoky spent untold hours developing that unique human dog relationship.

Sid's relationship with Chum was completely different. Chum never left the house where he lived. But once a week Sid would see Chum when he delivered milk with Bert the milkman. Chum's owner, Dan, was a milk customer and a good friend of Bert's. Bert and Dan played on the same soccer team. And Dan was always saying the reason why their team scored so many goals was because of Bert's powerful kick. Every Saturday morning Sid and

Bert would drop in for a cup of tea and a chat with Dan. It was during these Saturday morning chats that Sid would give Chum a friendly pat or two. It seemed that this was enough for Chum to take a liking to Sid and form their relationship—what there was of it. From what Sid observed, Chum didn't get too many pats of affection from Dan. So perhaps that's why Sid patted Chum as much as he did.

Then one weekend, an unusual, seemingly harmless incident occurred. This incident was the starting point of something, which, in later years, was to be the cause and topic of much conversation. While on the milk route, about half an hour after a cup of tea at Dan's place, the incident occurred. Chum appeared out of the blue and began following Sid and Bert. This was very unusual as Chum never left the house without Dan. Chum must have somehow or other slipped out of the house unnoticed. But because they had now walked quite a way from Dan's place, Bert wanted to keep going. Saturday was collection day and Bert didn't want to run late with his deliveries. Because of this, he decided he would take Chum back home on his way back to the milk depot. So they continued on their way delivering milk, with Chum happily following along. Then toward the end of the milk route, they reached Sid's house where Sid would knock on the front door and deliver the milk.

His mum, like clockwork, would come to the front door and pay for the week's milk. As usual, she opened the door to pay. But what was unusual about this day was Smoky was in the house. When the door opened, he just bolted out. During the whole time Sid had known Smoky, Smoky had never been inside Sid's house. But on this particular morning, Smoky had just sat on the front doorstep and wouldn't leave. So Sid's mum, knowing that her son would be along soon, let Smoky in. When the door opened and Chum saw Smoky they ran at each other like medieval knights in a jousting tournament. And what a crash it was. It was ferocious. They had never seen each other before. There wasn't the usual circling around as dogs often do to sum each other up. They just went at it. Sid didn't know what to do. Bert had gone a few houses up the street to collect money from Mrs. Fisher, and her garden was surrounded by a high hedge so Bert couldn't see what was going on.

When Smoky bolted out, Chum was out in the street by the milk cart. By the time they collided, they were on the grass sidewalk in front of Sid's house. It was here that the dogfight of dogfights took place. The fight went through three distinct stages. During the first stage both dogs were holding their own and Sid began wondering what he could do to stop the fight. He began by loudly shouting out their names. Usually this would have worked. But not a chance on this day. Then, he hopefully thought, perhaps when one of them had had enough, he would run off. But this was not to be. They were just going at it like two boxers toeing the line and punching it out. Neither was giving an inch. It was vicious.

During the second stage, Smoky started to show signs of fatigue and began backing away. But not Chum. It seemed as if he was just getting into his stride. It was then that Sid had an idea. He remembered reading somewhere that the way to separate fighting dogs was to pour a bucket of cold water over them. Sid didn't have a bucket of cold water. But he did have a milk cart with bottles of milk. So he quickly went to the milk cart and took a bottle and removed the milk cap. He then got as close as he could to the dogs that were madly snapping and biting each other. Then, when he saw his chance, he poured the milk over the dogs' heads.

While all this was going on, a crowd of at least a dozen people had been drawn to the fight scene and were causing a large commotion. But through all this ruckus, all Sid could hear was his mum loudly screaming, "Keep away from the dogs, Sid! You'll get bitten." Pouring the milk on the dogs was inconsequential. The fighting continued unabated. It was as if Sid had done nothing.

Then when the fight entered the third stage, it took a sad turn for the worse. Smoky was worn out. He was exhausted. He'd just had enough and capitulated. He pitifully lay on his side and literally stopped fighting. It was like a sign of submission, which Chum completely ignored. It was at this moment Chum showed his true self. He was a pit bull and Smoky never really stood a chance. When it came to fighting, Smoky was not in the same league as

Chum. Chum closed in for the kill. Blood was all over the place. Smoky's body was covered in blood. There was blood on the grass. Sid and some of the spectators had splashes of blood on their legs. The scene had turned ugly. Very ugly indeed.

Sid began to have an uneasy feeling and started to panic. He thought Smoky was going to die. There seemed to be no way to stop Chum. He had turned into an uncontrollable beast. As futile as it was, Sid continued to do the only thing he could think of. He turned to the milk cart and proceeded to get another bottle of milk. He was just about to remove the milk cap when he heard a loud yelp and a roar from the onlooking crowd. Sid quickly spun around and saw a beautiful sight to behold. He saw Chum running up the street as fast as his little legs could carry him. He was still yelping as he disappeared running around the corner.

Sid was confused and relieved. What had happened? Then he saw Bert. Bert just got back from Mrs. Fisher's and was looking at Sid with a half smile on his face. Sid let out a flood of questions. "What happened, Bert? Why did Chum stop fighting? Why did he run up the street yelping?" Bert's face now beamed into one big hearty laugh as he said, "I could see milk wasn't going to do the job, so I gave Chum a kick in the balls." Now it was Bert's turn to ask a question, "What the hell do you think you were doing pouring milk on the dogs?" After Sid had explained what he had read and tried to make his case convincing, Bert just shook his head in disbelief. It was as if Bert's head shaking was trying to say, "What's this generation coming to?" Many times after the event, Sid would think to himself, "It must have really looked pathetic, me pouring milk over the dogs. Especially when the milk poured so slowly." In retrospect, Sid could easily understand why Bert kept shaking his head.

It turned out Smoky wasn't dead after all, although he looked very much like it. Sid's mum fetched a blanket, and Smoky was gently lifted onto it and taken into the house. Sid wanted to help, but his mum told him, "Go and finish the milk route with Bert." When Sid did get back to the house, Smoky had been cleaned up but was looking lifeless.

Sid went around to see Smoky's owner. After explaining to the owner what had happened, it was agreed that Smoky would stay at Sid's house until he was ready to come home. Smoky recovered and lived for several more years. When he died his body was discovered in a place known as the spinney—a small area of trees and bushes. It was one of the places Sid and Smoky used to go to get away from it all. So Smoky's final deed showed that he must have really liked the spot.

A year later, when he left school, Sid stopped doing the milk route and never saw Chum again. For the rest of Bert's life, another forty years or so, Sid and Bert kept in touch. From the many hours on the milk route, Sid could recall many memories. Mostly happy and some not so happy, as the Smoky-and-Chum dogfight. But beside the dogfight, two other incidences stuck in Sid's mind, and they both had to do with Bert.

The first occurred when they were walking past the spot where the dogfight took place. Bert started to smile and Sid asked, "What's up, Bert?"

And Bert said, "I was thinking," and he paused, egging Sid on.

"What was you thinking, Bert?"

"I was just thinking, there are other things to kick besides soccer balls."

The second was when Sid turned up one Saturday morning, and Bert was all excited about a new product the Co-op Milk Company was selling. It was called yogurt. Now remember this was 1951. Britain was still getting over the war, and life was all about basics. And on the milk route it was about plain old milk. Although buying yogurt is nothing today, it was a novelty in 1951. It was sort of something special. It was new. You must also bear in mind in those days, nobody had a TV or a telephone. Whatever you looked at or heard was not trying to sell you something 24/7. But Bert was a go-getter. Besides his full-time job as milkman, he ran a part-time window-cleaning business. Two or three afternoons a week when he finished the milk route early, he would be up a ladder somewhere cleaning someone's window. Because Bert was such an aggressive salesman, he got down to business straight away.

He knocked on every customer's door to tell them what a new wonderful, healthy product it was. This took so much time that it added two hours or so to the milk route for the next couple of Saturdays. So one day Sid's curiosity got the better of him. He asked Bert the question that had been on his mind ever since they began selling yogurt. "Hey Bert, what does this yogurt stuff taste like?"

Without any hesitation, Bert replied, "Bloody awful."

Sid & Bert the Milkman

Sid & Bert the Milkman

Sid & Smoky - at the site of the dog fight

Sid & Smoky

Smoky - the dog that nearly died

STREET JUSTICE

IT WAS FIVE o'clock on a Sunday morning and the telephone rang. Barbara, who'd hit the pillow only three hours before, quickly grabbed the telephone and said, "Who's this?"

"Is that you, Barbara?" a quiet voice answered. Barbara recognized the voice immediately. With surprise in her voice, she said, "Is that you, Mum?"

"Yes, it's me, how are you, Barbara?"

"I'm fine, thanks, Mum. It's been years since we spoke. How are you?"

"I'm okay. I'm calling about your sister."

"What about her?"

"She committed suicide."

"Denise has what?"

In a voice that was louder and more assertive, her mother said, "She committed suicide."

"Why? Where? When? How?" Barbara quickly asked.

"It's too complicated to explain on the phone," her mother said.

Then in a pleading voice, her mother asked, "Could you come over?"

"When, Mum?"

"Right now, if you can."

"Right now?"

"Yes, if you can!"

"Okay, Mum. Let me make a few phone calls and I'll be over in about an hour or so."

"Thank you, Barbara. I'll be waiting."

It was easy, early Sunday morning, highway driving. Barbara brought the car up to speed, switched on the overdrive, put on her favorite music, relaxed, and began to think. The last time she had seen her mother and the family was about eight years ago at Uncle Phil's funeral. Since then she'd had no contact with the family whatsoever, not even a Christmas card. But she knew why. She was the black sheep of the family. She didn't fit in. She'd gone her own way and done her own thing and had done very well for herself. Here she was, driving the most expensive Jag money could buy, had a profession that she loved, lots of wonderful friends, and making oodles of money. Twenty years ago, she started out as a waitress working at a mediocre restaurant. Then through a combination of hard work, creating ideas on how to attract high-paying clientele, and using her good looks and charms, she was now the part-owner and head manager of a highly successful, nationally renowned nightclub.

Barbara then brought her thoughts back to her mother's telephone conversation. Denise, her only younger sister, had committed suicide. She couldn't understand this. Her sister seemed to have everything going for her. Denise was a dedicated nurse and was working on a Ph.D. which was to further her career in her field of—whatever it was, Barbara couldn't recall. *Why would she commit suicide?* Barbara pondered. Her sister always had a positive outlook. She had exceptional good looks and easily attracted people with her outgoing vivacious personality. As she exited the highway, Barbara said to herself, "I'm nearly there. I'll know soon enough what this is all about."

Her mind then started to tick off some of the old familiar scenes: same old potholed bumpy roads, garbage cans on the sidewalks, unused vehicles by the curbside, and too many houses needing a paint job. *Boy, am I glad I'm away from all this filth,* Barbara mused. "Here we are," Barbara noted, as she turned the corner, number 37, fifth house on the right. And there was Mum at the window, waiting, as she said she would be.

Her mother opened the door and never came out to greet her with hugs or kisses. Barbara wasn't hurt by this. Being the black sheep of the family, she was inured to the absence of family intimacies and sensibilities. But, more than Barbara expected, her mother's welcoming words were, "It's good to see you again, Barbara, and thanks for coming over so quickly."

"That's okay, Mum. It's good to see you again."

To which, her mum said, "How was the ride?"

"It was easy, Mum. There was hardly any traffic. So what's this all about, Mum?"

"Follow me, Barbara," her mum said, sounding more like an army sergeant than a mother. There was no "Can I take your coat?" or "Would you like a cup of tea or coffee?" There was just "Follow me," which is what Barbara did.

As she followed her mother, her mother looked straight ahead and talked. "I got up early this morning to go to the bathroom, and just as I was going back to bed, a thought came to my mind."

"What was that, Mum?"

"I thought I should take some dirty clothes down and put them in the washing machine."

Barbara was puzzled and becoming a little impatient. She'd had only three hours' sleep, cancelled appointments, driven quickly for an hour to see her mother, and all Barbara wanted at this moment was to know about her sister Denise. And all her mother was doing was prattling on about putting dirty clothes in the washing machine.

Then her mother said, "When I reached the bottom of the stairs, I found my baby." Barbara stood and froze. There was Denise hanging from a beam. Encircling her neck was a scarf. Her eyes were staring wide open upward. There was a chair on the floor that had been kicked away at the moment of self-execution.

Questions and thoughts started to buzz around in Barbara's head. She assumed, when she spoke to her mother, that Denise was in a funeral home or in a hospital or somewhere else, but not in the house. She never realized that Denise had so recently committed suicide.

"Have you called the police, Mum?"

"No. Before they take her body away, I wanted you to see Denise hanging here."

"Why would you want me to see Denise hanging there, Mum?"

"I will tell you later, Barbara. In the meanwhile I'll call the police."

The police came and were there all day. They sealed of the crime area, removed Denise's body, searched the whole house for fingerprints, questioned the mother, and filled in lots of paperwork. When the police were gone, Barbara decided to sleep over so she could talk to her mother about the suicide and catch up on family news.

After Barbara and her mother had eaten dinner and were comfortably settled in, Barbara asked the questions that had been on her mind all day. "Mum, why do you think Denise committed suicide? And why did you ask me over?"

Her mother quickly responded, "First, I know why she committed suicide, and second, I wondered if you could help me and the family out?"

"Of course, I'll do anything I possibly can. But please explain yourself, Mum."

Her mother replied, "It all happened two weeks ago. Your sister and a few of her nurse friends went to a party at the house of the world-renowned surgeon, Dr. DeLaney. Have you ever heard of him?"

"No, Mum, I haven't."

"Well, he's highly respected in the medical community and, according to Denise, some of the nurses refer to him and quote him with godlike reverence."

"Okay, Mum, so what happened?"

"Well, to make a long story short, he took her to a quiet part of the house and raped her three times."

"Are you sure of this, Mum?"

"As sure as we're sitting here, Barbara. Denise told me what happened at least a dozen times. He threw her on a bed and stripped her. The more she struggled and protested, the more excited and aroused he became. After he raped her, he wouldn't let her dress herself or leave the room. Then he raped her two more times. She was never the same again. From that day on, she started to mentally lose it. She couldn't sleep and wouldn't eat or drink. Then this morning, she took her own life. Denice was not streetwise like you, Barbara. As you know, Denise was in some ways very naive."

"Mum, did you go to the police and make a complaint?"

"I did. They said we could bring charges, but in the end it would be her word against his. Even with DNA evidence, the man would always say the act was consensual. Because of what the police told me, I never brought any charges. I also went to see an attorney, and he told me the same story. Without witnesses, there is no case."

"What about her friends?" Barbara said. "Didn't they see her all shook up and stressed out?"

"They'd all gone home by the time Denise left the party. They did say, though, they'd seen her with the doctor and she seemed a little woozy from drinking."

"Okay, Mum, that's really, really horrible what happened to Denise, but how can I help you?"

"Well, you manage that famous restaurant, that is, if you don't mind me saying, that is infamous for its clientele being somewhat on the other side of the law."

"Yes, Mum, that's true. But all my staff and I do is supply our clients with topnotch service, food, and drink, and after-hours entertainment. In return, they pay us handsomely and are never any trouble to us."

"Yes, I appreciate all that," said her mother. "But you must know someone who can help us."

"Mum, I never get involved in their business. Once you do, they have a hold over you. You'll always owe them a favor and your life is never the same again. But Mum, what is it you exactly want?"

"Justice. Street justice, if it has to be. I've tried the conventional methods of getting justice, and it's got me nowhere. Perhaps there's an unconventional way?"

"Exactly how?" Barbara asked.

"I would leave that up to your clients. They're the experts."

"Mum, you don't know what you're asking of me. But let me think it over."

On the ride out to see her mother, Barbara's thoughts had been on why her sister had committed suicide. Now on the ride home, she knew why and all the salient facts. But now her thoughts were on something else. Did she want to get involved to help her mother and the family out? It was a serious decision that could affect her way of life.

Several nights later, she knew the answer. Joe, whom she had known for a long time, came to the club for dinner. He was one of her favorite customers, and she knew he was also fond of her. Where he stood in the hierarchy of his business she didn't know. And never asked such questions. But she knew he had seniority by the way his associates addressed him. It was while he was there her gut feeling told her Joe was her answer. She was going to confide in Joe and ask him if he could help her and her mother. To do this, Barbara took Joe to her private office.

Joe listened very carefully. When Barbara had finished, he thought for a while. His first concern was for Barbara. He deeply valued their relationship because he liked the fact that she wasn't involved in his business affairs. With concern in his voice, Joe said, "You do realize if further steps are taken, you will be crossing the line. You'll be in debt to us for this favor. And you know what that means?"

"Yes, I do, Joe. And that's why I thought, when you do ask whoever you talk to, you could tactfully suggest that you would be repaying us for all the favors we have done your organization over the years."

Joe looked puzzled. "What do you mean, Barbara?"

"Well, for nearly twenty years, hundreds of your associates have had thousands upon thousands of quality, relaxing, entertaining hours from our services. I know we've been well paid, but we've never taken advantage of your generosity, and many times you got more than your money's worth, especially regarding late-hour entertainments. You know what I mean, Joe?"

That's what he thought was special about Barbara: that creative mind of hers. "All right, Barbara, this is not my area of expertise, but I know a man who has quite a reputation for solving such problems. I'll go and see him and put your problem and proposition to him."

A few days later in a different part of the city, Joe met the problem solver—the man known as the fixer.

"How are you, Joe? Haven't seen you for a while."

"I am very well, Mr. Cohen, and yourself."

"Good, thanks. You told me on the phone that you have something to ask me."

"Yes, I do. Take a seat, Joe, and let me know what's on your mind."

He took a seat and in Mr. Cohen's state-of-the-art office, Joe laid out everything Barbara had told him.

"Well, that's interesting. We'll be paying her back for all the favors she and her club has done for us over the years," chuckled Mr. Cohen. "Do think this is true, Joe?"

"Well, it's true. Our people from all over the country have had untold pleasures at her club."

"Sounds like I should go there myself, Joe," joked Mr. Cohen. But then he added, "Joe, we're not a philanthropic organization, but this Barbara has made an interesting point about us paying her back for all her club's services over the years. Come and see me Friday morning, Joe, around ten o'clock, and I'll tell you what I think."

"Yes, Mr. Cohen."

"Have a good day, Joe."

Joe left the office and Mr. Cohen started to think. "Let's see," said Mr. Cohen, "what did Barbara and her mother exactly want? They wanted justice. Street justice. What does that exactly mean in this case? Let's go to the Old Testament," said Mr. Cohen to himself. "It states, 'An eye for and eye and a tooth for a tooth,' which means, whatever a person did committing a crime should be equally done back to him. Which," mused Mr. Cohen, "is ironic, because the Golden Rule says basically the same thing, but, of course, it means something completely opposite, 'Do unto others as you would have them do unto you.' So how does that apply in this case? The doctor raped a girl three times. So he must be raped three times. A life ended up expiring. It's true she took her own life, but it was a resultant of his actions. So his life has to expire by his own hand." For a few days, Mr. Cohen gave the facts some thought and then called Joe.

When Joe sat down again with Mr. Cohen, Mr. Cohen got straight to the matter.

"Joe, I have decided how we're going to handle this. But before we set the wheels in motion, this lady Barbara has to do two things. She has to go and see her mother and tell her that they are absolutely never to discuss this suicide business on the phone, by email, by Tweeting or in writing. They can never talk about it in their homes or cars. They can only talk about it in a crowded area where there is background noise. You see, Joe," Mr. Cohen explained, "after this business is all over, some bright detective may put two and two together. He may connect Barbara's club with us and the suicide. It's unlikely, but you never know. They won't have any evidence, but they may start bugging telephones to get some. They're very good at this stuff."

"Yes, Mr. Cohen, I fully understand," said Joe.

"The second thing is, I need an up-to-date picture of this Denise woman."

"Yes, Mr. Cohen. I'll get on it right away."

A week later, Joe dropped the photograph off at the office. After Joe had left, Mr. Cohen looked at the photo and commented to himself, "What an attractive woman. What a sad waste." He then picked up the phone and dialed a memorized number. Mugsy.

"Yes, Mr. Cohen?"

"I have a job for you. Can you come over right away?"

"Yes, sir, I'll be right over."

Dr. Delaney was awoken by a voice crying out his name. "Dr. Delaney, are you there? Dr. Delaney, are you with us?"

As a surgeon, Dr. Delaney knew he'd been chloroformed. Although still drowsy, he could recall what had happened. He was in the hospital car park getting into his car when he was strongly grabbed from behind. After that, he couldn't remember a thing. But now his thoughts were returning. He could make out he was sitting on a very comfortable armchair. Then through his bleary eyes, he could vaguely see a man standing about ten feet away. The man was calling out his name.

"Yes, I'm here," answered Dr. Delaney. "Yes, I'm with you. What's this all about? Who are you? Where am I?"

"All in good time, Dr. Delaney. All you need to know is, my name is Mugsy. When you're ready, ring the bell on the wall. The butler will bring you a late dinner and after a good night's sleep, he'll bring you some breakfast in the morning. Then after you've had breakfast, I'll come and see you."

Mugsy left the room and Dr. Delaney began to appraise his surroundings. He was impressed. It was an executive, high-class condominium with top-of-the-line furniture and modern state-of-the-art restroom facilities. Then he began to wonder, *What's this all about?* Then he hit on what it might be. Some rich, high-society woman wants an abortion. That's it! They need my surgical skills and it all has to be hush-hush and confidential. He'd heard of this sort of thing before. But where does this Mugsy guy fit in? He doesn't seem to be a high-society type. Then the doctor superciliously chuckled and thought to himself, *I've never had a Mugsy come to one of my cocktail parties.* It was then, because of his self-assuredness, he realized he was feeling back to his old self, so he rang the bell.

The dinner was completely to his satisfaction. The steak was a tender filet mignon cooked exactly to his liking. The salad was fresh and tasty, and because the blueberry pie with cream was so delicious, he had a second helping. Whatever his apprehensions may have been, they left him as he lay on the bed and went to sleep.

Upon awakening, he could see that someone had been in the room. Fresh flowers had been placed in different parts of the room. The curtains had been drawn, and the morning sunlight pleasantly lit up the room. After seeing to his morning ablutions, he rang the bell, which was promptly answered. He was given a choice of breakfast. He was not a big breakfast eater, so he chose coffee and toast. Although everything was quality and comfort, he noted that the door was always locked when the butler left the room.

Well, it won't be long now. I'll soon know what this is all about, he thought, as he picked up and began to read the *New York Times.*

He heard the door unlock and looked up to see Mugsy coming into the room.

"Good morning, Doctor. Is the service to your liking?"

"Yes, except I'm locked up like a prisoner."

"I'm sorry, but that's a necessary precaution. I have a question to ask you and some things to tell you."

"Be my guest," said Dr. Delaney confidently.

"Have you ever seen this woman?" Mugsy asked, as he showed the doctor a picture of Denise."

"No. I can't say I have," the doctor replied.

"Now, come on, Dr. Delaney. You and I and a few other people know you have spent some intimate hours with this woman."

The doctor now realized that he'd not been brought here for his surgical expertise.

"What's this all about?" the doctor demanded.

"This, Dr. Delaney, is to do with justice."

"What do you mean, justice?"

"You've heard of an eye for an eye and a tooth for a tooth?"

"Yes, of course I have," said the doctor.

"Well, we're going to begin with a rape for a rape," said Mugsy.

"A rape for a rape. What are you talking about?" said Dr. Delaney.

"Mr. Super Surgeon, you raped this young woman three times and because of this, she took her own life."

On hearing this, the doctor was completely taken aback. He was unaware of the suicide. The doctor tried to get his mental bearings. What was the connection between this guy, Mugsy, who is obviously a gangster, and this nobody nurse who'd come to his party? How was he going to get out of this? He decided to come clean. He hoped his version of the story would clear things up.

"You're right, Mugsy. I've seen her, but only once. We met at one of my house parties. We had a few drinks and one thing led to another. You know how it is, these things just seem to happen?"

"No, I don't know how it is," said Mugsy. "I don't know how raping a woman three times just seems to happen, unless you're sick."

"Well, I have to admit," said the doctor, "I was a little rough with her, but she did seem to be enjoying herself."

"So why the suicide?" asked Mugsy.

"I don't know," replied the doctor.

"Well, I'm going to tell you what I know," said Mugsy.

"And what is that?" inquired Dr. Delaney.

"At eight o'clock tonight, three men are coming to pay you a visit, and the reason for their visit is exactly what this matter is all about."

"And what exactly is this matter all about?" queried the doctor.

"They're going to do something that's very rare," said Mugsy.

"And what is it that's so rare?" asked the confused doctor.

"They're going to administer justice."

"And how are they going to do that?" the doctor quickly asked.

"It's simple," said Mugsy. "You raped this woman Denise three times, and they're going to rape you three times. Each one is going to rape you once. And this is going to happen at eight o'clock every night until this business is over."

The doctor was aghast and horrified.

"You won't get away with this. I'm a doctor of international fame."

"Hold it, hold it," said Mugsy. "What did you just say?"

"I said I'm a doctor of international fame."

"No, no, before that."

"I said you wouldn't get away with this."

"Look here, Mr. Silver Spoon, Super Surgeon, thousands of people like me get away with things like this every day. It's a way of life for us. Now, I know every now and again politicians get tough on crime so they can get more votes. Surveillance devices are used to collect evidence, which has successfully put some of our top people away. But us unimportant soldiers on the ground, we're still here doing the daily business and getting away with it. So, Dr. Delaney, for us it's business as usual."

In nanoseconds, thoughts began to race through the doctor's mind. "I'm rich. I have prestige. I travel the world. I have front-row seats for the big fights. I can have any woman I want. I wear the best clothes. I associate with who's-who in the world of high society." Then his thoughts came back to reality.

"What can I do to make amends?" pleaded the doctor. "Do you want money? I have lots of money. I can see to it that you and your boys will have enough money for themselves and their families for the rest of their lives."

To this, Mugsy replied, "Dr. Delaney, I have lots of money. But what's more important is I have enough money. In other words, I don't need your money, and neither do my boys."

"So how can we come to some agreement to end this?" asked the doctor.

"Oh that's easy," said Mugsy. "You can end this any time you like."

"How can I do that, Mugsy?"

"Well, when you can't bear being raped anymore, you can just jump out of the window. This is the twenty-fifth floor. Then when your body's splattered on the sidewalk, it will be three rapes for three rapes and a suicide for a suicide."

Although the doctor was absolutely petrified of what was in store for him, he could see the logic behind it all. Someone, he concluded, has put a lot of thought into this. The three times he raped her plus her suicide would equal the three times that he's raped plus his suicide.

Then, in desperation, the doctor had an idea. Pleadingly, he asked Mugsy, "Can I jump out of the window right now?"

"No. Definitely not," replied Mugsy.

"Why not?" demanded the doctor.

To which Mugsy answered, "If I allowed you to do that, it would only be partial justice. You haven't been raped three times yet. What we want and will have is full street justice!"

GRANDMA'S EYEBALL

IT WAS THANKSGIVING and it seemed that everyone from our connected families had turned up this year to celebrate at our house. All the kids seemed to be having the time of their life. My two kids, Susan and Tommy, were teasing their younger cousins as they chased them around the living room. While the adults, who were forever conscious of kids flying by their legs, had separated into cliques. Not that the cliques intimated any animosity toward the other cliques; it was just the way it was. People who hadn't seen each other for a year or two or perhaps more were just catching up with latest family news or having a great time gossiping. Then there was my indefatigable, loving wife Rita who was constantly shuttling between the kitchen and the living room. When in the kitchen, she was single-handedly cooking Thanksgiving dinner for eighteen people plus making her dessert specialty: apple pie. Then, when in the living room, she was displaying her social skills.

I had a different and much easier social purpose of butterflying from person to person or group to group. On arrival at a person or group, it was my function and pleasure to see if their taste buds were content with whatever they were drinking and eating, and that the quantity of whatever they were eating and drinking was sufficient. Looking around and surveying the happy scene, I thought, *When this splendid bunch of people wake up tomorrow morning, they are going to collectively think,* "That was a great Thanksgiving dinner." Upon thinking this, I was suddenly taken back thirty years to when I was seven years old and at another family Thanksgiving dinner.

Thirty years ago, I was at one of Grandma Nell's Thanksgiving dinners. Everyone and everybody connected to our family went every year to the same location for Thanksgiving dinner: Grandma Nell's. It was a family rhyme that was said, "If you ever told a fib to Grandma Nell, she could always tell. And after that, your life was hell."

Whether this was true or not, I don't know, but everyone loved Grandma Nell. There was always a large, animated, diverse crowd at Grandma's Thanksgiving dinners. She had been organizing them for years, and in the family it was sort of a given that this is where everyone went for Thanksgiving. She really was quite a character and some would say a bit of an oddball. She was ninety-something with nobody really knowing what the something was. I and everyone else were left spellbound by her jokes and storytelling. Later, I came to realize how wise and shrewd a person Grandma was. As she was ninety-something and I was only seven, she was obviously psychologically leaps and bounds ahead of me. But because she was from the Great Depression era, she would tell me detailed stories of how stark and hard times were back then. These stories made me realize, relatively speaking, how much easier life had become for our generation, even though most people often moan and groan about something. And today, I am convinced that Grandma knew that her storytelling would bring me later happiness through the contrasts revealed by her stories. But however much I was fascinated by her storytelling, I was even more fascinated by one other thing about her: her artificial eyeball.

You see (no pun intended), Grandma Nell was blind in one eye. And in the blind eye, she had an artificial eyeball. Now, a lot of people are self-conscious about such things and the last thing they want to do is draw attention to it. Not Grandma. She seemed to get a kick out of seeing people squirm and be aghast when she removed the eyeball from her eye socket and casually plonk it on the table. She would then usually roll it around the table and laugh. Then she'd look around to see what sort of impression she was making on people. Most people felt uncomfortable about seeing her eyeball being plonked on and rolled around the table, but not me. The more I saw her do it, the more fascinated I became. You see, I was looking at it from the point-of-view of a kid. And one of the things I did a lot of as a kid was play marbles. Every time, I saw the eyeball rolling, I visualized myself playing with it as a marble. I could see myself rolling her eyeball toward another marble. Then, after it struck the other marble, it made a clicking sound. Soon, all I could think about was how I can get my hands on Grandma's eyeball so I could feel what it would be like to play marbles with it. I couldn't really say, "Hey, Grandma, can I have your eyeball and roll it around the table?" Well, I guess I could have done, but I just didn't have the nerve or audacity to do so, especially to Grandma Nell.

Well, I didn't have to wait long for my wish to come true. About an hour or so after one of Grandma's eyeball-plonking sessions, I had to go to the bathroom. And there it was, staring at me from the side of the washbasin. Grandma must have washed the eyeball and left it there. Now, I knew she had a bad memory, but I didn't know it was that bad. Even so, she might remember and come back, or someone might tactically tell her, "Grandma, you're walking around one-eyed." Then she or someone may soon come looking for it. This meant that I had to get out of Dodge double-quick because I wanted to try it out as a marble. After gently putting the eyeball in my pocket, I quickly made my way to an out-of-the-way room where my bag and things were, including some marbles.

As it turned out, the eyeball was harder than I thought it would be. It ended up making quite a good marble. To test it for playing marbles, I first rolled it on a linoleum floor until it gently struck a wall some six feet or so away. I repeated this several times, going a little harder each time. When I was convinced that I could use it as a marble, I picked out one of my marbles that was approximately the same size as the eyeball and began playing marbles with the eyeball. This was done by first rolling my marble until it became stationary, usually stopping five to ten feet away. Then I would take aim and roll Grandma's eyeball at my marble. The eyeball would either strike my marble, roll pass it, or fall short. If it struck the marble, the eyeball was given a score of one point. If the eyeball rolled, passed, or fell short, then it was my marble's turn to be rolled at the eyeball. This continues as long as you want, then scores are compared. Well, the game wasn't played long enough to see whether my marble or Grandma's eyeball had the highest score. There was a cacophony of voices shouting out, "Grandma's lost her eyeball! Grandma's lost her eyeball!" I could hear the voices getting louder and closer. It was time once more to get out of Dodge. I again put the eyeball in my pocket and made a run for it. Where to go and how to get rid of the eyeball was the question.

I dashed down the hallway and suddenly found myself in the kitchen. It was small and crowded with helpers who were too busy to take any notice of little ole me. I began looking around for a suitable place to hide the eyeball. I looked in some drawers and cupboards, but none were to my liking. Then, as I was passing the stove, I saw my aunt Sis stirring a pot of vegetable soup. She was my favorite aunt, so I decided to stop and have a quick chat with her.

"Hi, Jimmie, how are you doing? Are you, like everyone else, looking for Grandma's eyeball?" she said.

"No, Aunt Sis, I'm not," I quickly answered.

"I'm surprised," said Aunt Sis. "Grandma's offered fifty-dollar reward to whoever can find it."

"She is?" I answered, "I didn't know that. Fifty dollars!" *Wow! Fifty dollars for her silly old eyeball*, I thought.

Then my mind began to think contrasting thoughts. Grandma could be up to one of her tricky tricks to find out who took her eyeball, or *she could just genuinely want her eyeball back. What should I do?*

I decided not to take any chances with Grandma Nell, as tempting as the fifty dollars was. I was going to unload Grandma's eyeball, but the problem was, where? It was then that I observed some small onions in Aunt Sis's vegetable soup. They sort of resembled Grandma's eyeball in size, shape, and texture. So without dwelling too much on future consequences and making sure that Aunt Sis wasn't looking, I quickly took the eyeball from my pocket and surreptitiously deposited the eyeball into the pot of soup. Then, as nonchalantly as I could, I made haste out of the kitchen.

It was about an hour later that consequences began to rear their ugly head. Thanksgiving dinner was called and everyone quickly sat down around a long rectangular table. Grandma Nell was of course at the head of the table, with me seated about midway down. Grandma Nell was sitting there glaring at everyone with her one good eye. And her other eye, the one with the empty socket, was also glaring at everyone because it was open for all to see. It wasn't even covered with a patch. The atmosphere for a Thanksgiving dinner was, to say the least, subdued.

The first thing to be served of course was Aunt Sis's soup. Aunt Sis was especially proud of her vegetable soup and had been making it for Grandma's Thanksgiving dinners for as long as I could remember, which I have to admit is not very long since I'm only seven years old. And because Aunt Sis felt the way she did about her soup, she would go from person to person and personally ladle the soup from the serving bowl into their soup bowl. This was when things began to become interesting for me. From the beginning of Aunt Sis's ladling, I was watching very carefully to see if I could see the eyeball drop into one of the soup bowls. A couple of times I thought I did, once in Uncle Bert's bowl and then another time in Aunt Lil's. But because the flow of the soup was too quick, I couldn't really be sure.

When everyone was served, protocol gave us all permission to start eating. And dive in we all did. Because the soup was so delicious, most people were gobbling their food up so fast that it looked as if they had not eaten for days. This, of course, made my job doubly difficult. I was both watching if the eyeball was in my soup and at the same time looking around the table wondering who was going to find it in their soup bowl. When I had nearly finished my soup and could see the eyeball was not in my bowl, and also because most of the others had finished theirs, I was beginning to wonder if the eyeball somehow or rather wasn't in the serving bowl. Then there was a loud shriek. It was from my cousin Pam who was sitting directly opposite me.

She had her hand up by her mouth and was holding something in it that no one else could see. Even though I could not see what she had in her hand, I knew what it was. Now, my cousin Pam is usually composed and has her act together. But for a few brief moments, Grandma's eyeball tested her composure and got the better of it. From what she told me afterward, she had felt something in her mouth that was too hard to be a vegetable and had removed it to take a look at it. What she saw was an eyeball looking at her—Grandma's eyeball—and she shrieked. But perhaps remembering the fifty-dollar reward, she quickly composed herself and turned toward Grandma and said, "Grandma, I've found your lost eyeball." From which Grandma calmly replied, "My good eye can see that. Come here, Pam, and collect your fifty-dollar reward." So Pam went up to the head of the table and got her fifty-dollar reward. Immediately, you could feel the tension that had been hanging around the dinner table recede. People began to laugh more freely, talk louder, and were less inhibited. Even Grandma's two dogs could sense that the social atmosphere had become more relaxed. They seemed to be barking more and were running around with their tales wagging faster than ever.

But all of this merriment came to an abrupt halt when Grandma Nell started saying something in a loud voice. "Jimmy, come up here," she shouted. What was I to do? I was cornered. I couldn't run away. I stood up and slowly walked to the head of the table, conscious that everyone was looking at me. They were probably wondering, like me, what's this all about. When I got to the head of the table, she spoke extra loud so nobody would miss a word of what she was saying.

"Jimmy, because you are my favorite grandson, I'm asking you if you would you do me a big favor."

"Sure, Grandma, anything to help you."

"Well," she said, sarcastically, "you do know that I have not been able use my false eye for a couple of hours."

"Yes, Grandma."

"Well, I fear that I'm a bit rusty, so I need someone who I can trust that can help me put it back in the empty socket. Would you help me, Jimmy?"

Even the most gossipy of the gossipers were dead silent. There was not a rustle to be heard. This was Grandma Nell at her best for getting people's attention. I was also dead silent for a while. I was thinking of nice things to say, like "I might drop it" or "I might hurt you." But I realized that all of this sounded corny and insincere, so I bravely said, "Sure, Grandma, show me what you want me to do."

"That's my boy," she said. "Now, I know you are right-handed so come here and stand close to my right side. This will make it easier for you when you have to reach across and put the eyeball in my left empty eyeball socket."

I did as she said.

"Good. Everything all right, Jimmy?"

"Yes, Grandma." Although I was feeling what it must have been exactly like for the soldiers in the First World War. You see, I had just read about it. When a sergeant tells the soldiers to climb out of the trenches into no-man's-land, they must feel as frightened as it is possible to be. That's just how I felt: petrified and frightened.

"Now," Grandma said, "I want you to hold the eyeball between your thumb and index finger, so the eye is facing away from me, like this.

She gave me the eyeball, then watched me as I slowly positioned it as she had instructed me to do.

"That's me boy," she said again. "Now, don't be frightened. I'm watching you with both eyes." She gave a little giggle at her own joke, but it didn't amuse me.

With her left hand, she held my right wrist. Then, she slowly positioned my right hand so the false eye was in front of and correctly oriented toward the empty socket.

Now, I was feeling terrible. If she had not been holding my wrist, I think it would have been shaking. There wasn't a murmur from anyone sitting around the table.

"That's me boy," she said again. "Steady as she goes. You can do it. Get ready to push the eyeball in. When you hear a sucking sound, you will know it's home, safe and correctly inserted."

Oh no, I thought, *what if I push it too hard, or too soft, or too much to the right, or too much to the left?*

Then, in a flash, as quick as a wink, in what seemed like the speed of light, Grandma Nell took the eyeball from my hand and inserted it into her empty eyeball socket.

"There," Grandma said, "I guess I haven't forgotten how to play eyeballs. Thanks, Jimmy. I didn't really need you after all."

There was bewilderment and disbelief from the onlookers around the table. It was classic Grandma Nell.

Fast forward thirty years. As I looked around the room on Thanksgiving Day, I thought about all the people I had ever met or read about in my life, and came to the conclusion that there was no one more charismatic, amusing, and unpredictable as my Grandma Nell.

THE DEADLY SLEEPING BAG

JANET'S HUSBAND, FRANK, was unemployed, watched TV most of the day, drank too much beer, frequently took drugs, occasionally went with other women, but worst of all, he was a wife beater. Janet and Frank grew up in the same street and were childhood sweethearts. They were parents to three healthy, spunky, lovable children. Frank may have been a deadbeat husband, but he was a loving father. He was always taking the kids to the park, playing with them in the yard, and generally was a wonderful dad. Because of this and their long relationship, Janet found it difficult to leave Frank. But her feelings toward Frank had waned. She no longer had the crazy infatuation she once had for him. Although she tolerated most of his faults, the beatings were becoming more and more unbearable. On many occasions, when the beatings were especially bad, she had called the police. One time, Frank spent a night in jail, but he was only charged with being drunk and disorderly. So what could Janet do about the beatings? This was the big question she kept asking herself for years.

Then she got her answers from two TV shows. The first was when she heard a boxing trainer say, "Every man, at some time or other, lets his guard down and is vulnerable." The second time was on a TV program about bullying. The expert being interviewed said, "All bullies are cowards at heart. If a bully is seriously confronted, he will never bother you again." With these two insights, vulnerability and confrontation, plus adding an idea of her own, she came up with an answer that would end Frank's bullying once and for all. Because the answer was so simple, Janet knew it would work. Now, Frank wasn't a bully in the usual sense of the word. He wasn't always beating her up. He only beat her when he got badly drunk. And when he was badly drunk and passed out, he was vulnerable. Therefore, Janet reasoned that she could then give Frank the hiding of his life and he would never beat her again. Whether he would or wouldn't beat her again was a gamble she was prepared to take.

For her plan, the one thing Janet had in her favor was she knew exactly when to expect a beating: it was the first Friday of every month. On these Fridays, Frank and his buddies would go to a local bar to play cards, drink, eat, tell jokes, and talk about the old days. Even though Frank was unemployed and had no money, his buddies always paid for his food and drinks. He was popular and always had plenty of jokes to tell. It didn't bother Frank at all that his friends paid without there ever being any reciprocity on his part. That was Frank's nature.

Now, once again, Janet was waiting for Frank to come home. It was another first Friday, but this first Friday was different. Janet was going to put her plan into action. But first she had to undergo a beating. She knew this from the outset, but it was part of the plan. It had to seem to Frank that this was like any other Friday night out with the boys. On these Friday nights, Janet would either wait for Frank upstairs in their bedroom or downstairs in the kitchen. She preferred the kitchen because there was less chance of the children hearing anything. But more importantly, for tonight, she didn't want the bedsheets and covers disturbed. However, because tonight was going to be a night like no other night, she gave the kids a Grandma night. The kids were to stay over with Janet's mother. So with the kids out of the house, everything was in place for the plan. All it needed now was for Frank to come home.

It was just before one o'clock and Janet was waiting in the kitchen. Frank should be coming through the back door at any moment. Depending on how much he had to drink, her beating would range from being very severe to none at all. Because she had spent weeks anticipating this evening, she wanted the beating to be severe. Because the more severe the beating, the drunker Frank would be. And the drunker Frank was the more vulnerable he would be after the beating was over.

Waiting for Frank this Friday seemed an eternity. But after ten minutes or so, Janet heard a noise in the back alley. From previous first Fridays, she had got to know the telltale signs of how drunk Frank was. And tonight, the telltale signs were that he was quite drunk. First, he was fumbling and cursing trying to open the back door. Second, as he closed the back door, he slammed it loudly. And third, as he came down the passageway into the kitchen, his footsteps were slow and shuffling. He then came into the kitchen and saw Janet.

True to form, the first thing Frank did was to start ranting and raving about how the world had treated him unfairly. Janet had heard it all before. He blamed his parents for the way he was, the government for his unemployment, the politicians for the way the country was being run. But worst of all, he blamed Janet for ensnaring him into marriage. It was always the same self-pitying lamentations before the beatings started.

From previous beatings, she had learned two important things. If she tried to defend herself by fighting back, Frank would go berserk. The beating that then followed would the worst of the worst. So her plan was to move around the room as best she could and block the blows with her arms. She also knew that if she fell to the ground, Frank would continue the beating by preventing her from standing and kicking her. Because she especially didn't want to be kicked, she planned to defend herself in the standing position as long as she could. She hoped by then that Frank would tire himself out and go upstairs to their bedroom.

Then the beating began. She knew by his aggressiveness that tonight was going to be a bad one. Frank came at her hard and fast, punching wildly at Janet's upper body. She had rested up and was prepared. She quickly backed away and blocked the first round of blows. This didn't bother Frank, who continually kept moving forward and punching. Finally, Janet's defenses broke down and she took punches to the jaw, nose, and left eye. Because Frank was right-handed, Janet tactfully focused more on his right-side attacks. But in the end, Frank's power overwhelmed her. But she was not yet completely out of the fight. Janet was determined not to go down to the floor until Frank started to show signs of tiredness. And this she managed to do. After about two minutes or so, Frank started to breathe heavily. He suddenly lowered his arms, muttered a few obscenities, and left the kitchen. Janet could now hear him stumbling up the stairs as he made his way to their bedroom.

Janet was like a trained athlete. She expected a severe beating. She had prepared for this and knew exactly what she was going to do. First, she had to assess her injuries and then rest. The injuries looked worse than they felt. Her nose was bleeding profusely, her left eye was blackened, and her jaw was aching. Both her arms were hurting from defending the punches. She knew in a few hours that they would be covered in bruises. It had happened before. After bathing her nose and putting cotton wool in her nostrils, she put some ice around her left eye. Janet then lay down on the living room sofa and rested. This was to prepare herself for the physical exertions that would soon be demanded of her. She pressed the set button on the alarm of her cell phone. The setting was for two hours. It had previously been set. It was all part of the plan.

Upon awakening, Janet took assessment of herself. As expected, she was hurting, but she felt ready for the task ahead. She refreshed herself with a large drink of cold water and made her way upstairs to the bedroom. And there he was. As the boxing trainer had said, "Every man lets his guard down sometime and is vulnerable." Frank, lying there sound asleep after one of his nights on the booze, was a man with his guard down, and Janet meant to take every advantage of his vulnerability. When Frank lay down on the bed and tucked himself in, he had no idea he had unwittingly become part of Janet's plan. Using her sewing skills, Janet had sown the lower half of the bedsheets together. In the upper half, she had sewn on a zipper, which was presently unzipped. This left the bedsheets open, allowing Frank access to get in between the sheets when he got into bed. Janet now calmly and methodically zipped the zipper up Frank's right side and over the top of his head. She then calmly walked around to the other side of the bed and zipped the zipper over the other side of Frank's head and down his left side. Frank was now trapped inside in what can best be described as a large deadly sleeping bag the size of a king-size bed.

Janet then knelt down and pulled out a baseball bat from underneath the bed. This wasn't any old baseball bat. It wasn't some lightweight baseball bat that kids played with. This was the real thing that the pros use. Janet had shopped around and had made a point of buying the biggest and the best one she could. Again, all part of the plan.

With the baseball bat in hand and standing at the side of the bed, Janet relished the moment she had long been waiting for. She then wielded the bat high above her head and swung it down as hard as she could, hitting Frank somewhere on the upper part of his body. Then, working herself into a frenzy, she hit him again and again and again while shouting, "You bastard, you bastard, you bastard!" If ever there was a Shakespearian moment of "Hell hath no fury like a woman scorned," this had to be it. But after about ten or fifteen seconds, she suddenly realized that she was terribly out of breath. The vigorous, frenzied actions were too much for her body to endure. The beating she had taken and the lack of sleep over the past few days were beginning to tell on her. She didn't have the endurance to continue at this pace.

This wasn't part of the plan, she told herself. *I have to rest for a few minutes. I have to keep control of myself.*

It was then that Frank started to speak. "Janet, what are you doing?"

"Shut up," she snapped at him.

But Frank wouldn't be quiet and begin to say, "But Janet," and before Frank could utter another word, wham, Janet hit him with the baseball bat with all her might. There was now silence from inside the bedsheets. Janet then lay down on the bedroom carpet. Collecting her thoughts, she realized she must take her time. There was absolutely no reason to hurry. There was only her and Frank and this given moment in time, plus the baseball bat.

Janet now resumed the beating using a completely different strategy. It was going to be cat and mouse. Instead of continually hitting Frank on one spot, she was now going to switch from one part of Frank's body to another. The blows would be just as hard, but the time between blows would be much longer. This way, she wouldn't tire so quickly. Also, Frank wouldn't be able to defend himself, because like a mouse with a cat, he wouldn't know where the next blow was coming from. Because the sheets were opaque, Frank couldn't see Janet, but Janet could make out Frank's outline, which made it easy for Janet to decide where and when to aim her blows. With Frank lying on his side, she began at his feet with two blows in quick succession, then one on his knees, then two on his shoulders. With Frank screaming for mercy and beseeching Janet to stop, Frank rolled over onto his front and curled up in a fetal position. Janet pummeled his back and buttocks. He then rolled over onto his back and tried to protect his body by wrapping his arms around his bent-up legs. Janet then hit him on his knees and feet. Wherever Frank rolled, there was no escape. She hit him here and she hit him there, but she didn't hit him everywhere. She never hit him on the head or around the head area. She paid special attention to this. She didn't want to kill him. She just wanted give him the battering of his life so he would never think of beating her again.

Janet lost all track of time as she continued the cat-and-mouse beating. As far as the plan was concerned, she really hadn't considered time. She thought she would stop beating Frank when she'd had enough. But instead, it was Frank's inactivity that brought the beating to an abrupt end. Suddenly, he wasn't moving or screaming anymore. Janet stood by the side of the bed for a minute or so. She decided against unzipping the bedsheets to see how bad she had battered him. Instead, Janet calmly walked over to the corner of the room and stood the baseball bat in the corner. She then went downstairs and called the police.

She introduced herself as Mrs. Janet Stacey from 26 Walnut Street.

"Yes, Mrs. Stacey, I know who you are," replied the policeman. "Has your husband been beating you again?"

"Yes," she answered.

"Do you want us to come over?"

"Yes, please."

"Okay. We'll be right over."

In about five minutes, the doorbell rang. Janet opened the door and recognized the two policemen. They had answered some of her previous calls.

"Wow, I guess he's been at it again,' said the policeman, as he looked at Janet's black eye and the cotton wool protruding from her nostrils. "Are you well enough to answer a few questions?" he asked.

"Yes, sir. In fact, I haven't felt this good in a long time," Janet replied.

The two policemen looked at each other with puzzled looks. They thought she must either be losing it or making fun of them.

"Where's your husband? Has he run off again?"

"No. He's upstairs."

"Upstairs?"

"Yes, on the bed upstairs. Let me show you."

The two policemen followed Janet upstairs to the bedroom.

After Janet led them to the bed, they both just stood and stared. First, down at the bed and then at each other. What they saw was a crumpled body under bloodied bedsheets. They couldn't see the body but could make out its human shape. Without being Sherlock Holmes, they guessed it was Frank, her deadbeat husband.

"What happened?" asked one of the policemen. Janet didn't say a word but just pointed to the corner where the baseball bat was. For the second time that night, the policeman said, "Wow!"

But this time, the wow was far louder. Taking control of the situation, one of the policemen said, "There are two things we have to do. We have to call an ambulance for your husband, and take you down the station and book you."

"Yes," said Janet, "I completely understand."

The ambulance arrived in minutes. The medics who came were veterans at emergency work and had seen it all before. That was until they unzipped the sleeping bag bedsheets. More wows, followed by good heavens. After weighing up the situation, one of the medics commented, "If it hadn't of been for Janet and Frank's size disparity, the outcome of the incident would have been far more serious." Meaning, Frank would probably be dead! Frank was a few inches over six feet weighing 230 pounds, and Janet was five feet seven weighing 155 pounds. When the medics and police were finished, Frank was taken to the emergency room and Janet to the police station.

At the police station, the police reviewed their records. Over the past five years, Mrs. Stacey had called the police department on thirty-seven occasions. Everybody knew there had been other beatings, which she'd never reported. The problem was, Janet never pressed charges. She always hoped the beatings would somehow go away, but they never did. In fact, they became regular. Because of this, she did what she did and was prepared to face the consequences. The charges against Barbara were serious, but because of her thirty-seven recorded beatings and someone had to take care of the three children, it was decided to let Janet go home. She had to sign a few forms agreeing not to leave town until the whole matter had been legally sorted out. It was also agreed that after Frank had been released from hospital, he was to stay at his mother's house to recuperate.

Now, an unusual turn of events began. It was a perfect example of the law of cause and effect. One thing happened after another that, as it turned out, blessed the good fortunes of everyone involved. It all began at the police station. The news of what Janet had done spread like wildfire. Most policemen were sympathetic to Janet's plight and admired the ingenious way she had got even with her husband. They also admired her pluck and daring. The policemen from the local precinct knew policemen from other precincts, and it wasn't long before every policeman within a fifty-mile radius knew of the event. Because of this word-by-mouth news, a local newspaper picked up the story. Several reporters came to Janet's house and interviewed her. The next day, her story was front-page news showing an article and two pictures. The article explained in detail all that had happened. One picture showed Janet with her three children and the other showed a close-up of Janet's face that amplified her black eye.

Then a local TV station contacted Janet. Because her story was so unique to the community, they asked her if she would do a live TV interview. Janet hesitated. She didn't mind being interviewed in her own home, but in front of cameras and an audience while answering ad-lib questions, she has no experience whatsoever in presenting herself to the public. She told them that she would think it over. Two days later, Janet was contacted by a national TV station. They were very enthusiastic. They thought her story had national appeal. They offered Janet two hundred thousand dollars for a one-time appearance before a sixty-million prime-time live audience. The two hundred thousand dollars took her off guard, but another plan was forming in her mind. She asked if they would wait a few days before she gave an answer. The new plan needed cooperation from Frank, who was still recuperating in hospital. So Janet decided to take the bull by the horns and go and see Frank and work out a deal with him. With this done, she would then be able contact the national TV station and negotiate her terms.

When Janet approached Frank's bed, she was shocked at what she saw. Frank had lost the use of both hands and arms and was being intravenously fed. His face was covered with bandages with two openings for his eyes and one for his mouth. Because he had lost some teeth, he had difficulty talking. So he just nodded his head whenever he wanted to show agreement or disagreement. Janet got straight to the point and put her proposition to him. She told him that a national TV station wanted to interview her on prime-time TV to a live audience. She made it clear to him that it was her they wanted to interview and it was her they had contacted. But she said, "After all you have been through, I thought you should have a chance of making some money. All you have to do is sit on the stage with me. You don't have to do or say anything. If you do this, you will be paid fifty thousand dollars."

On hearing this, Frank's automatic reflexes went into action, and he sat bolt upright, just as Janet had thought. Frank jumped at the idea of making easy money. He nodded his head in agreement. To a lowlife like Frank, fifty thousand dollars was a huge amount of money. He once got spasmodically excited over the chance of winning fifty dollars at a bingo game. For fifty thousand dollars, he could easily put aside his machoism and sit on a stage next to his wife. For fifty thousand dollars, he didn't mind being looked at by millions of people while being covered in bandages from the beating his wife had given him.

Janet now broached the subject that was closest to her heart: divorce. She told Frank that none of this can happen unless they get divorced.

"It's up to me whether you appear on TV, and it's up to me whether you get the fifty thousand dollars."

Because she could not see his face, she couldn't judge his body language. And until she asked more questions, she didn't know how he would respond. Janet continued, "Frank, you have a chance of getting fifty thousand dollars. You can see the kids on weekends or whatever other arrangements you like, but only if we get divorced. If you say no, then I go up on the stage alone and you don't get any money."

Janet kept pushing the money aspect because she knew that a lowlife like Frank was more persuaded by money than anything else. Even so, this was a tough one for Frank. He had been brought up as a strict Catholic and divorce was a big no-no. What would his mother say and her family? But the fifty thousand dollars was the deciding factor. And Frank began to think of all the things he could do with fifty thousand dollars: "I could buy a brand-new fancy car, take my buddies out drinking, go on a Caribbean cruise." Frank's mind became delirious with runaway thoughts of what he could do with fifty thousand dollars. Of course, Frank hadn't a clue how quickly fifty thousand dollars could melt away once you start big-time spending. So he acquiesced to Janet's plan by nodding his head up and down. But to ease his conscience, he thought to himself, *All I have to do is go to confession. The priest will say a few Hail Mary's and everything will be all right.*

"Okay," said Janet, "if it's all right with you, I'll have the attorney draw up the papers." Frank nodded his head in agreement.

Janet now called the national TV station. She told them she would do the live interview but only if her husband was up on the stage next to her and she wanted two hundred fifty thousand dollars, not two hundred thousand dollars. This came as a bit of a surprise to the sophisticated managers of the national TV station. Having a husband-beating housewife dictate the terms of a contract was not the usual way they did business. It was they who usually dictated the terms. It's true that Janet was taking a gamble, but current events were on her side. There had been a lot of activity in several women's movements regarding wife beating. Also, bullying had become a current issue and was regarded as an overlap to wife beating. So women's rights, human rights, wife beating, and bullying all combined together in Janet's favor. A David-and-Goliath story of a wife beater being beaten up by his wife promised to be an exclusive TV interview. The national TV station agreed to Janet's demands.

In order to make the interview as dramatic as possible and show the plight of women's rights in the best possible light, it was decided that Janet would be interviewed first.

Frank would then be brought on the stage at the appropriate time. Janet had told the story of her turbulent marriage so many times that telling it and answering the interviewer's questions were easy. But when she spoke about her plan to get even with Frank, it wasn't so easy. She spoke hesitantly, sometimes giving the feeling that she had been too severe with Frank and was beginning to doubt herself. Perhaps she was conscious of the fact that the audience had not yet seen Frank, and when they did, they may be appalled by what she had done. Janet explained in detail the whole plan: from preparing the bedsheets into a sleeping bag, enduring the beating, zipping Frank up in the bedsheet sleeping bag, beating Frank with the baseball bat, being taken to the police station, and the police answering her thirty-seven telephone calls. In the audience, there were plenty of women's rights supporters. When she described herself being beaten by Frank, there were deep sighs from the audience. Then, when Janet described how she pummeled Frank with the baseball bat, there was a spontaneous outburst of applause, which then removed any doubt in Janet's mind about her plan being in the wrong.

Because he was unable to walk, Frank was wheeled onto the stage. Some bones in his feet had been broken and one knee had undergone serious surgery. Both arms and wrists were in casts as were most of his fingers. His face was covered in bandages and, as mentioned previously, slits were cut out for his eyes and mouth. He also had some broken ribs. His body, which at one time was totally covered with bruises, was by now either fully or partially healed. Frank was now able to talk as his broken teeth had been fixed. A reporter, who was present at the time, reported that Mr. Stacey looked like someone who had been in two car accidents, each happening one day after the other. The protagonist in this TV special was supposed to be Janet, but on arrival, Frank took center stage. People just couldn't keep their eyes off him. Even when the interviewer or Janet were talking, the audience was transfixed on Frank. Before the eyes of millions of people was this diminutive mother who had beaten the living daylights out of her beefy husband. It was an historical moment in the world of feminism, and Janet and Frank were testimonials to this. Janet, again, became the protagonist as the audience began chanting, "Hip hip hurrah for Janet! Hip hip hurrah for Janet!"

The interviewer quickly calmed the audience down and resumed the interview. Originally, Frank wasn't going to speak, but because his teeth had been fixed, he asked beforehand if he could say a few words. Janet and the interviewer had agreed. So now it was Frank's turn. The interviewer gave him the floor by asking him what he had to say about all that had happened. You could have heard a pin drop. What was Frank going to say? What Frank said surprised everyone, especially Janet. Frank said that he had been doing a lot of thinking. He now realized that he had treated Janet awfully. And on reflection, he couldn't understand why Janet had put up with him for so long. He also had a message for any wife beaters who may be watching. He told them, "Give up beating your wife. Wife beating is a habit that some men resort to when everything seems to be going wrong. Your wife and family are the greatest treasures you'll ever have, and that's all I have to say." The audience wasn't expecting this from such a monster. At first, the audience was silent. Then someone started to clap and then a few more began to join in. By and large, the audience was subdued, but Frank had got Janet thinking about their divorce.

After two months, Frank was discharged from the hospital and was convalescing at his mother's home. As Frank still couldn't walk, Janet and the kids visited him twice a week. And during these visits, Janet was beginning to have second thoughts about the divorce. He seemed changed. He wasn't such a know-it-all and his arrogant bossiness was gone. And there were the kids. Having a father during childhood was far healthier than not having one at all. What was she to do? Well, Frank answered the question for her. On one of his visits to the hospital, Frank lost it. The nurse who was changing his face bandages accidentally did something that caused Frank excruciating pain to his jaw. Frank still couldn't use his hands or his left arm, but he could now use his right arm. And because the nurse was standing close to him, Frank was able to encircle his right arm around her neck. He then proceeded to squeeze and strangle her. While doing this, he was shouting out how useless she was as a nurse and would never again see the inside of another hospital. Fortunately, there were two male nurses present who quickly overpowered Frank and literally saved the nurse's life. That was it for Janet. She told the attorney to finalize the divorce papers.

Meanwhile, requests for interviews continued but were diminishing, so Janet decided to do one more interview and then call it quits. There was a good turnout and the interview went well. But after giving interviews for over a year, this interview, like so many others, ended up being routine. That was until the Q&A portion. A young girl asked Janet what the greatest satisfaction she had experienced from the whole affair. Janet thought, *What an interesting question. During all my interviews, no one had ever asked me this before.* She thought for a while and replied, "You've all heard about turning the other cheek. Well, you can go and stick that up you know where. Because my greatest satisfaction was when I knew that my plan was going to actually happen: the day that I finished sewing the deadly sleeping bag."

Because the answer was so simple, Janet knew it would work. She got the answer from a TV program, although at the time she didn't know it. The whole family was watching a title fight and the champion was the favorite to win. The challenger's trainer was being interviewed and he was talking about the challenger. The interview lasted several minutes and afterward Janet couldn't remember a thing he'd said. All Janet was waiting for was to see the fight. But a few weeks later, when she was thinking about her beatings, she amazingly recalled part of the interview.

It was, “Every man has a weak spot, and every man, sometime or the other, lets his guard down and is vulnerable.” When she’d first heard this, it went completely over her head. But later, when sublimely recalled, it made sense. When does Frank let his guard down and become vulnerable? From that moment on, she knew she had the solution to her problem. She knew exactly when and where Frank was vulnerable. The other TV program that influenced her had to do with bullying. On this program, a bullying expert was being interviewed. Because he was pushing his book, Janet wasn’t taking notice of what he was saying. That was until he caught her attention with, “All bullies are cowards at heart. If a bully is seriously confronted, he will never bother you again.” The program then followed up with several interviews of people who had been bullied. In every case, they said, “If a bully is strongly resisted, he will never trouble you again.”

WHAT HAPPENED TO IT?

IN 1963, I met an elderly gentleman named Fred who told me a wartime story about himself and his good friend Charlie. They were serving in the British Army during the First World War. I remembered and wrote the story some fifty years after meeting Fred. The story you're about to experience is told by Fred in the first person.

Charlie and I first met in 1914 in a British Army boot camp. It was here that we were being trained to kill Germans, or anyone else we were ordered to. Like millions of others in 1914, we had eagerly volunteered to fight in the First World War, also known as the Great War, or later referred to as the war to end all wars. Charlie was very special. He had a way about him that is difficult to describe, especially his sense of humor. Often he would say, "Fred, you're such a good shot with your rifle, you're going to kill more Germans than any other English soldier." Charlie was definitely ahead of his time for such a young person from a working-class background. Once you got to know him and he felt at ease in your company, he would reiterate about the evils of capitalism and its beneficiaries, the upper classes. He was prophetic, as many of the things he said turned out to be true. He said that when this war is over, nothing will change. The system of predatory capitalism will still be in place. The glutinous never-ending desire for money will be fed by more trumped-up wars, continual ups and downs in the stock market, and increases in taxes which always favor the rich. He said that this war and all wars are wars between the upper classes that use the working class as cannon fodder.

Charlie was a voracious reader and he got a lot of his ideas from his father. His father was involved in some way or other with the Labor Party. Charlie would often proudly quote that his father had personally known Kier Hardy, the founder of the British Labor Party. I told him I'd heard about the Labor Party, but like most people at that time, I didn't know too much about it. To which he would sarcastically reply, "Fred, how can you ever know anything with what you read? All you read is newspapers and they're all owned and controlled by puppets of the English aristocracy. Do you think you're going to read detailed articles in their newspapers on how the Labor Party's policies would raise the standard of living for millions of Englishmen?" When I heard him talk like this, I would usually say, "I don't know, Charlie, I haven't given it a lot of thought." From which he would always reply, "Fred, that's the way they want it. They don't want people to think. Especially thinking about a system that's unfair to the majority but not to the plutocrats who run it."

Well, there I was with Charlie and thousands of other soldiers on a ship going somewhere to do our duty for God, King, and country. It wasn't until later that we were told that we were going to a place called the Dardanelles, a place which I think most of the soldiers on the ship had never heard of.

Charlie and I had only been there a couple of hours when the sergeant said, "Fred and Charlie, I want you two lads go and survey the best place to dig some latrines." He pointed to a hill that was about half a mile away, which had some trees and bushes on the top of it. "Take some shovels with you and find a place that's private where the ground is not too gravelly or rocky for digging. The latrine has to be about four foot deep, two foot wide and about forty yards long. When you've found the best spot I'll have a look at it, and if it's okay we'll have ten men go up and get it dug as quickly as we can. Did you understand that?"

"Yes, sir," we said and saluted.

"Get going then and don't hang around."

So Charlie and I went up the hill to do some latrine surveying. We were to be the genesis for toilets for two thousand or so soldiers during the upcoming months. What a responsibility.

We had only been up the hill about ten minutes or so when Charlie said to me in a somewhat muffled voice, "Look down there." And coming up the hill was an officer. Not just any officer but probably the most disliked officer in the whole regiment. Some of the officers were really okay fellows, but this one was from the old school. His father was Duke somebody or other, and he was, we heard through the grapevine, always boasting about his family's blue-blooded, aristocratic heritage. The way he was coming up the hill, you could see by his body language that he was trying to find a private place to relieve himself. And don't mean urinate because he could have done that behind any old bush. What he was doing was looking down at the grass, which bordered the bushes, and occasionally looking back to see if there was anyone else coming up the hill behind him. Although he was the other side of the bushes to us, we were able to see him because we were higher up the hill. We could see him but he couldn't see us.

It was then that Charlie whispered to me, "We can have a few laughs here." And I thought, *how could we possibly have a few laughs with this despicable officer?* Well, I'd gotten to know Charlie in the last few months and I knew he had a mischievous, creative, quick-thinking mind. So for the sake of a laugh, I was open to listening to whatever he had to say. But all he said was, "Keep out of sight, keep quiet, and follow me," which I obediently did. First, we went back down the hill but circling away from the bushes that the officer was the other side of. This was to make sure that he never saw us. Then, when we got past where the officer was, we turned around, and went back closer to the bushes. With Charlie leading the way, we were now walking about ten feet away from the officer, who was on the other side of the bushes but diagonally ahead of us. When the officer stopped, we stopped, which happened several times. Each time he stopped, he would check the grass that bordered the bushes and look around to see if there was anyone coming up the hill. I was following Charlie as quietly as I could and at the same time keeping my eyes on the officer. But while all this was going on, I hadn't a clue what Charlie was up to. And I couldn't ask him because I was too scared that even the slightest whisper would attract the officer's attention.

Suddenly, Charlie raised his arm up, signaling for me to stop. I immediately froze dead still. The officer seemed to have made a decision. This was where he was going to relieve himself. He slowly unbuttoned his coat, carefully folded it, and laid it on the grass. He seemed to be in no hurry. Charlie, on the other hand, sprang very quickly but quietly into action. He lowered himself to the ground and, with his shovel positioned in front of him, began crawling commando style toward the officer. I couldn't believe my eyes. *What's he up to?* I thought. Then the unthinkable dawned on me. Is he going to do what I'm thinking he is going to do? No, he can't be.

But sure enough, just as he'd been trained to do in boot camp, Charlie continued crawling commando style toward the officer. The officer now unbuckled his belt, and while he was still looking around, he lowered his trousers down to his ankles and squatted in preparation to do his business. It was while the officer was squatting that Charlie smoothly and quietly pushed his shovel forward and positioned the shovel just between the officer's shoes and trousers. Then, as cool as a cucumber, Charlie waited for the officer's bowels to complete their function. The wait seemed interminable but it probably was no more than a minute or so before the bowels had done their job. With the officer's droppings now resting on the shovel, Charlie began a reverse commando crawl. It was during this time that I felt the most apprehensive. Charlie could have easily made a noise while crawling backward, or the officer could have looked down and seen the shovel. During all these activities, I held my breath in anticipation. Then I backed out of the way as Charlie got clear of the bushes and stood up. He said, "Let's get out of here."

Charlie led the way up the hill again so we could be in a position to observe the officer. Again, the officer didn't seem to be in much of a hurry because by the time we got in position, he was just finishing buckling his belt. It was then that the fun began. The officer looked down to cover his dropped business and there was nothing there to cover. What went on in his mind at that moment is anybody's guess. Now, here was a very educated person, probably Eton or Harrow, who had been doing this once a day for about twenty-five years and had probably consciously looked down at his business for twenty of those years. At a quick calculation, without taking leap years into account, this makes it about seven thousand three hundred times he has experienced looking down at his daily business. Now today, on his 7301st time, there is nothing there. That would be enough to make any man doubt himself and perhaps even go a little crazy. The officer then began circling around the dropping spot looking in every direction. He even looked up. Perhaps he thought it had floated away and his droppings were having some sort of religious experience! After about five minutes of this, he picked up his coat and walked down the hill. Charlie and I were beside ourselves with laughter.

"Look at this," said Charlie as he held up the head of the shovel, horizontally balancing the human excrement so it wouldn't roll off. "There's a message here, Fred. Do you know what it is?"

"A message? It's a piece of shit on a shovel!"

"No, no, no, no. This tells you, without a shadow of doubt, that the high and mighty does it the same as the low and the insignificant." Then Charlie said, "Fred, this is our secret. If word gets out about this, his revenge would have no limits, especially when you consider the influence of his family."

I completely agreed and said, "Charlie, mum's the word."

Charlie then swung the head of the shovel up and the dropping flew into the air. Then, as they were falling, he swung the shovel like a cricket bat and hit the droppings. They flew some twenty or so yards into a field of tall grass. The evidence was now discarded. After a while, when we'd finished laughing and reality began to rear its reliable head, I said, "I think we should get back the sergeant. He will be wondering where we are."

"Not so fast," said Charlie. "Don't be surprised if Mr. High and Mighty doesn't come back for a second or third look." And sure enough he came back two more times and circled around the dropping spot looking and looking but to no avail.

Finally, when we did get back down to camp to report to the sergeant, it turned out he wasn't there. He had been called away on some other business, so all my worries about him missing us had been completely unnecessary. While I was lying on my bunk that night, all I could think about was the amusing events of the afternoon. I believed that this was the end of the incident, but unbeknown to me, it was not to be the end of the story. The end of the story took place several years later in circumstances completely different from where I was now.

The war in the Dardanelles dragged on for about nine months and got nowhere. It was a catastrophe. After some five hundred thousand casualties on both sides, the powers that be in London decided that the fiasco was a failure and it was time to pack it in and bring the soldiers home. The returned soldiers would then be available to go and kill German soldiers on the Western Front instead of Turkish soldiers in the Dardanelles. It wasn't worded exactly like that, but the summation was the same. The main scene of the war, the Western Front where mankind had never before witnessed such numerous casualties, continued on for another two more years.

But during the last few weeks of the war, an event took place in England that put the nail in the coffin on the story of the lost droppings. For those soldiers of our regiment who happened to still be in England during the remaining few weeks of the war, there was the annual football match between the privates and the officers. This was all played in good fun with an unusual get-together afterward, where officers and privates could intimately socialize. This socializing of officers and privates was normally never done; it was even taboo. But the annual match made an exception of this. This year, I was an inside forward for the team and when I turned up, I saw none other than Mr. High and Mighty himself on the officers' team. I had not seen him since the hilarious event on the hill nearly three years ago. Someone told me the war had changed him. Some of his closest friends had been killed in the war and it seems he now had more empathy for other people. Well, the privates dominated the game and we won the match 4–1. I'm sure if it had been a cricket match, the result would have been a win for the officers.

Afterward, we all got together in the officers lounge where the officers and soldiers mixed and mingled over a few drinks. Mr. High and Mighty was at a table on the other side of the room but I was able to clearly observe him from where I was sitting. And much to my surprise, he was genuinely laughing and joking with the soldiers at his table. So I decided, when the opportunity arose, I would join him for a pint or two. Finally, toward the end of the evening, I got my chance when some of the soldiers left a little early. I managed to get a seat right next him and immediately began talking to him. First, I wanted to get a feel of the man so I talked to him about the game. As he played on the wing, I complemented him on his speed and how he often outran our halfbacks. Then I discussed with him the numerous times he had placed wonderful shots in front of the goal area. Although his shots were perfectly placed, his center players were not able to capitalize on the opportunities he'd given them. By now, officers and privates had broken into groups or talking one-on-one. As it turned out, I was in the latter group. I found myself having a really enjoyable conversation with the officer who I always referred to as Mr. High and Mighty. After talking about the game, we talked about the war, what was going to happen after the war, and he was particularly interested in my background—where I lived, went to school, what my parents did for a living, my brothers and sisters, and so on. But what was really on my mind was what took place up on the hill nearly three years ago. I know I had promised Charlie that mum was the word on this subject, but that was mum between me and the other soldiers. But if it was just between him and me and not the other soldiers, it wouldn't really matter. Well, that's what I persuaded myself.

After four pints of beer, I was feeling good. And the fact that I would probably be away from all this war business and back in civvy street in a month or so, I broke down. I broached the subject that had often replayed itself in my mind, which at this very moment was very strongly on my mind. I started gently to see how he would react. I said, "You probably don't remember me but I fought at the Dardanelles."

"Yes, I was there," he said. "Terrible mess. We lost so many good men there."

Then, still trying to be gentle and tactful, I said, as quietly as I could so as not to attract attention, "Do you remember the first day when you went up the hill to the bushes?"

Now, I had his complete attention. He started to sit up straight and stare at me. His face became ghostly white and his eyes opened wide, staring at me like a madman. "Go on," he said in a firm but inquisitive voice.

Hesitatingly, I continued, "Do you remember that you looked around for a while and finally found a private spot—" and before I could say another word, he strongly gripped my forearm with both his hands and began vigorously shaking it. As he was shaking my arm, he began shouting, with each shout growing in intensity and volume. He shouted, "*What happened to it? What happened to it? What happened to it?*"

Fast forward to 1963 when I met Fred, who shared the above story with me. He told me that the story was absolutely true. At the time, I was young. I was far more gullible and credulous than I am today. I believed every word he said, but as the years passed by, I began to have doubts about the story but I had no proof whether the story was true or not. With a stretch of the imagination, the story could have been true.

We now fast forward to 2017. This makes it just over a hundred years after the event and I am now eighty years old. My wife and I visited England to celebrate my eightieth with four English friends who were also turning eighty. While there, I told them the "What Happened to It" story. And one of my friends, Brian, who had spent his life being very active in the British Civil Defence Corps, told me that he had heard the same story but it did not involve an army officer but an Irish man. It seems as if this story has been doing the rounds for about a hundred years. By now, the protagonist to this tall tale has more than likely been, to name a few, a Welshman, a Scotchman, a Frenchman, a German, a Pole, along with many others, which I can leave to your imagination. As disappointed as I was with Fred, I had to admit that it made a good tall tale. It has stood the test of time for a hundred years and has probably brought laughter to thousands of people. So in the long run, is there anything wrong with that?

TED'S TEETH AND TESTICLES

WHENEVER ANYONE MET Mrs. Taylor for the first time, they would invariably say that she was a kind, genteel, and considerate person as she was. But on subsequent occasions, they would detect something they had not detected during their first encounter. They would realize this kind, genteel, elderly lady had a tough, no-nonsense undercoat to her public demeanor. It could be deciphered in the message of her words and the distant stare in her eyes. If someone really became friendly with Mrs. Taylor, they would discover that she had a very unusual eccentricity. But for them to discover this, they had to be invited to her home. On first entering, it would seem like any other home. But on entering the living room, visitors would see something on the mantelpiece that could only bring about a lengthy stare. They would not be able to take their eyes off it. They would see two glass jars: one containing a full set of dentures, and the other, two testicles.

The following story explains Mrs. Taylor's eccentricity of the two glass jars on the mantelpiece and the duality of her mental toughness and genteelness.

For many years, Mrs. Taylor, whose name is Cecil, was happily married to a man named Fred. Fred was an architect who worked for the city, so money was never a problem. Fred truly loved Cecil and doted on her. They had one son, Ted, and Cecil doted on him. So with financial security and all this doting going on, the family had many years of happiness. Then suddenly, out of the blue, while at work, Fred keeled over and died from a heart attack. At first this was devastating for Cecil and Ted, who was by now a teenager. But Cecil now showed her true mettle. Life had to go on. She continued her life as if Fred was still alive. She now, more than ever, focused her love, talents, and efforts on Ted. She did a wonderful job. He became an outstanding student and went on to college, where he obtained a degree in business, specializing in sales and marketing. He was a gregarious person with a penchant for sales. Because of these qualities, he was hired as a sales representative by a well-known medical company. As the years passed by, he became one of their top salespersons and was forever flying all over the world to close deals or give professional advice. He moved out of his mother's house and bought an upscale condominium two streets over from her. Because they lived so close to each other, Cecil would drop in and see Ted every day. It was during this time that Cecil's happiness was at its zenith. Seeing her son so successful was a tonic. What more could a mother ask for? But Ted had a problem. Not really a serious problem, but it was one that gnawed away at his equanimity. The problem was dentist visits. To say he was scared when visiting a dentist was putting it mildly. He had a phobia.

There was no explaining why or where the fear came from. He was petrified of even having his teeth checked and cleaned. So one day when he was in the dentist's office, he said to the dentist, "I want all my teeth taken out."

"You want what?" the dentist asked.

"I want all my teeth taken out," Ted emphatically replied.

"I've never heard of such a request, and why would you want such a thing?"

"Look," said Ted, "I have twenty-eight teeth left and that means, at a guess, I'll be seeing a dentist fifty to one hundred times in my lifetime. But if you take them all out, I'll never have to visit another dentist again in all my life. I'm not worried about the cost, just please take all my teeth out!"

The dentist thought for a while and said, "Why don't you think it over and give me a call in a week?"

"Okay," said Ted.

In a week, he called the dentist. Ted hadn't changed his mind. He wanted all his teeth out.

"All right," said the dentist, "but it has to be done over two visits."

So Ted went in for two visits, with each being two weeks apart. Ted was jubilant. Ted now had dentures, which meant he would probably never have to visit another dentist again in his life.

All went well with Ted and his dentures, except he did have one small incident about a year later. He was driving to the airport for one of his trips abroad when he realized that he had forgotten to wear his dentures. The reason for this was because he lived alone and he was in the habit of not wearing them at home. And with so many things on his mind and hurrying to leave the house and catch the plane, he forgot all about them. So he stopped the car, called and cancelled his business appointment, and went home. He then ordered another set of dentures. When he received the spare dentures, he put them in his car so he would never again be caught by his forgetfulness.

The next thing that happened to Ted of any physical consequence was that on one of his annual physical checkups, the doctor detected a small lump in his testicles. Although it checked out as benign, he was told to come back in six months for another checkup. On his return, it was found that the lump had grown, had spread to both testicles, and was malignant. So it was agreed that Ted had to have his testicles removed. The surgery went well with no complications. Then Ted made an unusual request. He asked his doctor if he could have the testicles to keep at home. The doctor thought the request was unusual, but he gave his permission. He told Ted that the testicles must be kept in a sealed jar, otherwise they would go moldy. Ted did as the doctor ordered and placed the sealed jar on his living room mantelpiece.

For several years, life was idyllic for Ted and his mother with their relationship being loving but not overbearing. While he was busy pursuing his career, she kept herself busy playing bridge and cycling with friends.

Then the idyllic existence came to an abrupt end. On one of his business trips, Ted's plane crashed, killing all on board. It was a small business plane with four passengers and a pilot. The plane was flying between small islands and crashed into the ocean. The wrecked fuselage was found, but no bodies were recovered. One can only conjecture how devastated Mrs. Taylor must have been on the news of her son's death. Bereavement from a death is bad enough to bear, but having no tangible body for a funeral service must have exasperated her grief. But once again, Mrs. Taylor showed her mettle. She decided that what she wanted was some physical reminders of her dearly beloved Ted. Not photographs, videos, or any of his favorite possessions. She wanted something personal so she could be reminded of him each day. She decided to place his spare dentures and testicles on her mantelpiece. It was bizarre. She wanted the teeth positioned in the jar to give the impression that they were smiling. With this done, the two jars were then positioned next to each other, giving the impression that the dentures appeared to be smiling at the testicles. With Ted's parts in place, life resumed a changed but tolerable existence for Mrs. Taylor. The weeks passed into months and the months passed into years.

Several years after Ted's demise, Mrs. Taylor decided to give her living room a new lease on life with new furniture. The furniture was expensive, modern, with a continental appeal. Two men delivered and set up the furniture for Mrs. Taylor. They, like everyone else, were taken by surprise when they first set eyes on the mantelpiece. They didn't say anything but they momentarily stared. They were just there to deliver and set up furniture, but Mrs. Taylor did not miss their stare. By now, she had got over Ted's death and immediately began telling the furniture men about her late beloved son. She told them everything: how good he was at school, his college qualifications, his company position, how he came about having all his teeth out, having his testicles removed, and she even told them how much money he was earning. It just all came out. She was a proud, loving mother. The furniture men were there for four hours on what should have been a two-hour job. Between assembling the furniture, listening to Mrs. Taylor, and the cups of tea she kept serving, the time flew by. They never got drawn into conversation with her. They just gave her understanding nods at appropriate times during her portrayals. But during these four hours, they could not help but note the overlapping, reciprocating qualities of Mrs. Taylor's genteelness and toughness.

When the furniture men were back in their van, the younger of the two turned to his experienced partner and asked, "What did you think of the old lady?"

"What did I think of the old lady?" he mused. "I think she's a sweet old lady with a lot of balls!"

THE LOST JUDO MAN

Once upon a time, there lived a man who was a judo fanatic. There are and have always been judo fanatics, but this man was so fanatical that others seemed merely enthusiastic compared to him. He was not a world champion, or an Olympian, or even recognized internationally. This was because he began judo in his late twenties—past his peak competitive years. But he did rate nationally and spent the rest of his life trying to catch up with lost time. He thought about judo day and night. During the day, he consciously applied his logic and reason to every facet of judo. During the night, his subconscious mind would decipher and interpret this logic and reasoning. He voraciously gathered information from books, DVDs, online, teachers, higher and lower grades, and anywhere else he could.

He would spend endless hours visualizing judo's four methods of scoring: one, throwing an opponent on to his back with force, speed, and control; two, immobilizing an opponent for twenty-five seconds with a hold; three, applying an armlock on an opponent until he submitted; and four, applying a strangle or a choke on an opponent until he submitted. Besides the four-method scoring, he would also visualize judo's three methods of training: one, practicing the form of judo techniques with a nonresisting partner; two, practicing the learned forms on a resisting partner; and three, test the techniques in the competitive environment of a contest. These three forms would be the same for a golfer: form—practice his swing; practice—have a round of golf; and contest—enter a golf competition.

Besides his visualization exercises, he was equally active on the mat. The school where he trained didn't churn out champions like some schools did. But geographically and practice-wise, the school suited his purpose. But to experience the teachings of other instructors and different styles of practice, he would travel far and wide and visit other schools. His school would sometimes have visitors that were Olympians or world champions. It didn't matter though who they were. When they ended up grappling on the mat with him, he was always able to apply a strangle on them. Such was his success and fame as a grappler that he was nicknamed and became known as The Strangler.

Other aspects of his life were his family and profession. Both were complete and successful, and would have satisfied the majority of people. But if the truth be known, he would have willingly traded them for his beloved judo. He was married to a wonderful woman, who was quite content to care for his everyday needs. She was completely aware of his innermost interests and tolerated his evening and weekend absences along with his hours of silence when he was studying judo at home. They had married young, long before he discovered the ways of judo. They had two children, who were married and live in different parts of the country. He was a chiropractor by profession. His practice was located in the center of town and known by everyone. He had a large clientele, and because of his business acme, he had a lucrative business. Over the years, the fanatic became a rich man. So with financial security and a settled domestic homelife, he lived a life contemplating and practicing judo. It seemed to him that his contented life was like the order of the universe—it would never change. But it did. He awoke one day to find his wife lying next to him with a calm, serene look on her face. It seemed to be a fine omen to the start of another good day, but it wasn't. She was dead.

The postmortem showed she died of a heart attack. This was strange because there was no family history of heart problems and her annual physical checkups showed her heart to be robust, with her blood pressure being normal. The loss of his wife was to have a catastrophic effect on the fanatic's life, although he didn't initially realize it. For the first few weeks after his wife's death, he was surrounded by family and friends, who took care of his everyday needs. It was when they left that the seriousness of the situation hit home. Because his wife did everything around the house, he hadn't a clue where things were kept, and when he did manage to find something, he usually didn't know what to do with it when he found it. For example, he searched high and low for a needle to sew on a button. When he found the needle, he didn't know where thread was kept. When he found thread, it took him about half an hour to sew the button on his jacket. His wife would have done it in less than two minutes. Now she was gone, he realized that his wife had done so many household chores, which he'd been completely unaware of. His wife cooked all the meals, washed the dishes, cleaned the house, washed and repaired clothes, did sewing, darned socks, paid the bills, did the shopping, cleaned the cars, serviced the cars, tended the garden, and did all the yard work, including removing leaves and shoveling snow. In summation, she had done every chore there was to do round the house while he was thinking about or practicing judo. In the beginning, it was difficult and embarrassing for the fanatic. His first week's breakfasts, lunches, and dinners consisted only of breakfast cereal and delivered pizzas. With the help of a few friends, he slowly but surely picked up the pieces. Forever reverting to his trained judo mind, he was always honest with himself. Only by being honest could he accurately evaluate his judo, and so it was with his new domestic life. From his honesty, he sadly concluded that around the house, he was a completely useless individual.

Besides all the things his wife did for him, she took to her grave a secret that only they shared. It was to do with his memory. Everyone forgets minor things, such as where they left the car keys or turning the heating down before leaving the house, but the fanatic's problem was concerned with major things. A year ago, they'd been on a vacation for four weeks. A week after they got back, he asked, "When and where are we going on vacation this year?" Even when shown the vacation pictures, he couldn't recall being away. After his son got married, he couldn't remember attending their wedding and having had dinner at their house on several occasions. These lapses in memory were mysterious. But what was even more mysterious was, he would remember each forgotten event about six months after it had occurred. It was like his mind was in a coma for six months and then he suddenly remembered everything. It was now about six months since his wife had died.

One morning, he woke up with a dreadful thought. He could see it all. He now knew why his wife had died. His mind could now recall the event with graphic clarity. His wife had got up in the middle of the night, and after returning to bed, she tucked herself in and pulled the blankets over her shoulders. Although half asleep, it was these movements that kindled the fanatic's thoughts. He was lying on his left side facing his wife, and his wife was also lying on her left side, so her back was to him. In his half-slumbering state, with a body moving in front of him, it meant only one thing. To the fanatic, he was on the mat grappling. Instinctively, he attempted to apply a strangulation technique from the rear. But before he could complete the technique, her body went limp. "This," he exclaimed, "is why she died from a heart attack." It was now all so clear to him.

"What have I done?" he wailed. "You utter, stupid fool," he shouted out aloud. He realized it was his fanatical, single-minded pursuit with judo, something that was impossible to perfect, that had brought him to this miserable situation. He had killed the most cherished person in his life. And it was only now, when she was dead and longer part of his everyday life, that he realized she was all he had. She was everything. He felt completely lost with nowhere to go. Not even judo could liberate or console him from how he felt. Mixed with emotions from the guilt of his dastardly crime and a future that seemed so bleak, it wasn't worth comprehending. The fanatic now felt a completely lost judo man. "Now, what am I to do?" he asked himself.

On pondering the possibilities, he realized that if he gave himself up to the authorities, they would charge him with either manslaughter or insanity. In either case, he would be institutionalized: sent to prison or a mental institution. The thought of living like a caged animal was an anathema to him. *I could run away*, he thought, but this was cowardly and not his nature. After thinking it over for a few days, he decided that there was only one answer—suicide. Being who he was, there was only one way to commit suicide—by strangulation. But the big question was, how would he do it? He wasn't going to jump off a chair in some cellar. That was too ordinary, and being ordinary was not the fanatic's style. Then he came up with an answer, which he named, “The Bungee Break.” It would be a bungee jump with a difference. Instead of a rope being tied around his ankles or waist with an elastic bungee cord, it would be with a rope noosed around his neck. The Bungee Break technically meant his neck would break; he wouldn’t actually be strangled. Because a free-falling body accelerates at thirty-two feet per second, it meant that after falling for two seconds, a body would have fallen or dropped sixty-four feet. As a precaution against the unknown, the fanatic experimented. He purchased a cadaver of his own weight and dimensions, noosed a noose around its neck, and using a seventy-foot long rope, he threw the dummy over a cliff. The body dropped for about two seconds and came to an abrupt stop when the rope became taught. The head remained intact with the body. He was now satisfied that a seventy-foot drop would break his neck and not decapitate him.

Before committing suicide, the fanatic put all his personal affairs in order. He paid his debts, he reviewed and updated his will, he left a lengthy goodbye note to his children, and said goodbye to judo friends and those chiropractic clients whom he had become close to. On the day of the suicide, two things were prevalent in his mind. First was the pact that he and his wife had made. They both agreed that if they knew they were going to die, their last thoughts would be on each other. Second, because neither of them believed in afterlife, arrangements were made that would ensure that their atoms would be intermingled together for eternity. In his note to his children, the fanatic had given instructions to have his and his wife’s ashes mixed in a jar and scattered on a lake. The lake was near a trail where he and his wife had spent joyous hours hiking. More joyous, he now realized, than his judo hours had been. They did not believe in death, only a change in the form their atoms would take after death. Having their atoms intermingled for eternity was a very comforting thought for the fanatic as he approached the cliff to make his Bungee Break jump. He knew he only had two seconds of free fall, which is a long count of 1001, 1002. He ran to the edge of the cliff and jumped. He then visualized himself and his wife together. He visualized her gentle, serene face from their younger, happier, carefree, idyllic years. Then the rope ran out of slack. His mind became instantly oblivious, and his body swayed backward and forward in the breeze as he dangled on the end of the seventy-foot rope. It started to rain and birds flew overhead. Life continued on: impersonal and detached.

THE LIZ TAYLOR LOOK-ALIKE

THE JUDO CLUB was situated in a now disused fifteenth-century church in the city of London. The sounds of chanting priests and singing choirs were now replaced with the sounds of breakfalls and cries from throwing exertions. The judo school had two dojos. The main dojo was located on the ground floor, which was mostly covered with forty by twenty foot traditional Japanese tatami matting. The remaining area housed an office and half a dozen spectator chairs. The second dojo was upstairs from the main dojo. It was small and used for private lessons and beginner's classes. Also upstairs were the changing rooms and showers. It had been another good night at the dojo. The forty-plus members who had attended the evening training session were now showering and getting ready to go home.

The members had spent the evening engaged in an exercise called free practice. This is a very challenging exercise where couples, while holding each other's judo uniform, maneuver around the mat, trying to throw each other using judo throws. The exercise is timed for five minutes. They are then given a one-minute rest period. During this time, they change partners and resume for another five-minute practice. This procedure continues until the end of the class. The physical and mental exertions from standing free practice can be exhilarating and exhausting, and sweating is usually profuse. Free practice is an exercise that improves throwing skills in a competitive environment. There are no winners or losers.

The dojo was now quiet but not empty. Two members, Ralph and Harry, had remained on the mat to put in some extra practice. Both were very experienced judo players and were currently in the British judo team squad, placing them among the top twenty judo players in the country. They were like the couple from the old TV series *The Odd Couple*. They were as different as chalk and cheese but were bonded by the sport and art of judo. This bond was cemented over the last three years by their three, four, or five times a week practices. Ralph earned his living as a hod carrier. He worked on construction sites where, using a hod, he carried bricks all day long, up and down a ladder, five days a week. This had made him very strong and fit and had given him extraordinary powers of endurance. Hand in hand with working on construction sites, Ralph's adjectives were replete with swear words. And at times, much to Harry's chagrin, Ralph could be very crude and vulgar. Contrary to Ralph, Harry was quiet, reserved, rarely swore, and was university-educated with a degree in economics. He worked in the city for a prestigious company as an accountant, with a dozen or so people reporting to him.

Before beginning their extra practice, Harry and Ralph were giving themselves a few moments' rest. It was during this time, when Harry was doing some stretching exercises, he heard Ralph say, "Gee, what would I give to fuck her?"

Harry, who couldn't stand hearing foul language, especially when on the mat, quickly turned around to confront Ralph when he saw a young woman of stunning beauty sitting on one of the chairs at the other end of the mat. Harry's thoughts of reprimanding Ralph's crude language were instantly forgotten. Harry's focus was now captivated on a woman who had momentarily taken his breath away. Like some of the women who worked in Harry's office, they would dress to keep up with the latest fashion or try to make themselves look like a particular movie star. But this woman wasn't doing either. She didn't have to because she looked exactly like Elizabeth Taylor. From head to foot, she was a Liz Taylor clone. She was wearing a very expensive, fashionable, light brown, suede dress that hugged her petit, shapely figure. The dress came down to a few inches above her knees and she was sitting with her legs crossed. Besides the impeccable physical traits that Harry observed, it was her elegance that made the greatest impression on him. She was sitting completely relaxed with an air of self-confidence that, to Harry, was the mark of an aristocratic upbringing. An upbringing with privileges that imbues the privileged with an absolute air of sophisticated self-confidence. After Harry's mind had calmed down, he began to wonder: Who is she? Where did she come from? What was she doing here in this out of the way dojo? But one question that kept repeating itself was, who is she waiting for? Harry made a quick mental run through of all the club members. Most were teenagers and she's probably not waiting for any of them, unless she had a brother. But as far as he could judge, they were too rough and ready for her. There was one man in his late twenties who he'd heard was training to become a doctor. Perhaps it's him? Then there were a few men in their early forties. Perhaps one of them was her father. But again, it didn't fit. They didn't seem to fit her social class. His piqued curiosity was interrupted by the sound of Ralph's voice. "Hey, Harry, I've got an idea."

To appreciate and understand Ralph's idea, the reader has to be aware of the nature of the extra training that Harry and Ralph were about to undertake. Instead of standing practice, which the class had been doing all the evening, they were now going to practice the wrestling aspects of judo. They were going to grapple and wrestle on the mat, trying to apply the mat work or groundwork scoring skills of judo. There are three such scoring skills. First: holding skills. Here, one person is immobilized and unable to escape from the applied hold. Second: choking and strangulation techniques. Here, restriction of air or flow of blood to the brain results in a hand-tapping signal of submission from the person being choked. Third: armlocking techniques. Here, pain applied to the elbow joint results in a hand-tapping signal of submission from the person being armlocked. While wrestling or grappling with each other trying to apply these three skills, they could either roll around a few square feet of the mat or they could roll all over the mat. It all depended on the situations that occurred through the give and take of the two participants.

Harry had now regained his bearings. He was again thinking about the extra practice he and Ralph were about to engage in. He said, "Okay, Ralph, what's this idea of yours?"

"Well," said Ralph, "do you see that girl over there?"

"Yes, of course I can see her."

"What if you and I roll around and work our way over there and see what we can see?"

"What do you mean, see what we can see? We can see her from here."

"Yes, of course we can see her from here, but if we got closer, we could see up her skirt."

"Ralph, are you sick or something? What's seeing up her skirt going to do for you? Anyway, she's got her legs crossed, so you're not going to see anymore over there than you can see from here. By the time we get there, she may have uncrossed them," Ralph quickly replied. Harry had had enough of this foolishness. It was completely contrary to his way of doing things. He was just about to say, "That's it, I'm bowing out. I'm going for a shower. We can do some extra practice another night," when Ralph said, "Come on, Harry, we don't know when we'll get this opportunity again." These words triggered a thought in Ralph's mind. Of the many times they had done groundwork practice, Harry had never scored on Ralph. He'd sometimes held him down for a few seconds with a holding technique. But because Ralph was as strong as an ox and had such phenomenal powers of endurance, Harry was never able to come close to getting Ralph to submit to a choke or armlock. But, Harry thought, *perhaps with Ralph's mind being so obsessed with looking up this girl's skirt, he had this once-in-a-lifetime opportunity of getting the better of Ralph.* Ralph was right; we don't know when we'll get this opportunity again. So Harry decided to go along with the stupid idea.

"Okay, I'm in," said Harry.

"I always knew you were a sport," said Ralph.

"But under one condition," Harry strongly asserted. "We don't make it obvious. We start at this end of the mat and stay up here for several minutes before we make our way down. Then after moving down a bit, we stay there for a while and so on until we get to the other end of the mat."

"That sounds perfect to me," Ralph excitedly added. After performing a kneeling salutation to each other, they stood up and Harry threw Ralph to the mat. The throw was not resisted but was just a practical means of beginning the mat work practice. And so the practice began. It was quite a tit for tat. Both had turns in gaining and losing advantages. Harry was surprised that Ralph didn't seem to be focusing so much on the beauty at the other end of the mat as he expected him to. In fact, it seemed to Harry, Ralph was trying just as hard as he normally did, except once when they were about halfway down the mat. Harry was on top and both were looking toward the Liz Taylor look-alike. Ralph suddenly froze their movements and said, "Can you see anything?"

"No, I can't see anything. There's nothing to see."

"Okay," Ralph said, "Let's keep moving."

So they continued down the mat until they were about three feet away from the ravaging beauty when Ralph suddenly said, "That's it, let's stop." He stood up and walked over to the empty chairs. Harry, who was very strict on judo protocol, became irritated. Ralph hadn't even bothered to finish the practice with a bowing salutation. This had never happened before. While still irritated by this and bewildered by the sudden stopping, he heard Ralph say, "Harry, I'd like to introduce you to my fiancée. Harry, this is Mildred. Mildred, this is my good friend, Harry."

Then, with the broadest Cockney accent Harry had ever heard, the Liz Taylor look-alike said, "Glad ter meet ya, Arry. Ow ya doin? I've erd all abou ya!"

ABOUT THE AUTHOR

Sid Kelly worked as an engineer for fifty five years designing high speed automation assembly machines and production equipment — pens, razors, lighters, glass and medical equipment and more.

For over sixty years, he has practiced, competed, studied, and written about the martial art of sport judo. He was in the British judo squad and represented Great Britain on nine occasions in international matches (1965-67). He was head instructor of the Renrukan JC that produced three British Team players. He captained the Northern Home Counties (NHC) team winning the Area Team Championships (1966), and won Britain's first kata championship at the NHC Area Championships (1965), and passed the National Coach Award Examination first time.

Sid emigrated to the USA in 1967. He was overall winner of the New England Judo Black Belt championships, two times Connecticut State Champion. He was owner and head instructor of a judo and karate school for 10 years that had 200 + members. He was an active national referee for ten years. He produced three videos (70 applications of the arm lock Waki-gatame)(1990-1995), and 5 DVD's (multi-choice testing on 110 techniques)

(1995-1996). He was two times gold medalist in the Worlds Masters Judo Championships (Canada 1999) (Japan 2004), and coached the winning Connecticut Judo Team in the United States Judo Association (USJA) National Team Championships (1999). October 16th was declared SID KELLY DAY in appreciation of his judo services to the town of Milford, Ct. (1999). He was awarded the rank of 8th degree black belt (2005). Certified as a personal trainer, Certified USJA Coach, Certified Master Examiner, and Certified Kata Examiner. Chairman of the USJA Promotion Board (2008-2013) — rewriting and updating the USJA Promotion Manual. For thirty five years he was on the teaching staff at Americas oldest judo camp — the NY YMCA International Judo Camp. Published 'Judo Poems' (2009). Created, tested, and copyrighted a system that introduces new students to the skills needed to competitively apply throwing techniques (the 5 steps to standing randori)(2010 - 2018). Created 3 types of standing practices (randori) and 3 types of judo contests: for beginners, recreational players and the athletically inclined (2018).

In retirement he gives judo clinics, reads, writes, teaches English as a second language, belongs to a health club, and attends a writing club.

He lives with his wife Rita in West Haven, Ct, USA. They have two children, Susan and Tom, and three grandsons, Beau, Atticus, and Thaddeus.